The Overnight Ordeal

Books in the Choice Adventures series

THE OVERNIGHT ORDEAL

Karen Ball

Tyndale House Publishers, Inc.
Wheaton, Illinois

Library of Congress Cataloging-in-Publication Data

Ball, Karen, date
    The overnight ordeal / Karen Ball.
      p.   cm. — (Choice adventures ; #16)
    Summary: The reader's choices determine the course of the adventures of a
group of Christians as they confront various fears while spending the night in
the belltower of their church.
      ISBN 0-8423-5134-5
    1. Plot-your-own stories. [1. Plot-your-own stories. 2. Christian
life—Fiction. 3. Adventure and adventurers—Fiction. 4. Fear—Fiction.]
I. Title. II. Series.
PZ7.B19880v 1994
[Fic]—dc20   93-40182

Printed in the United States of America

99 98 97 96 95 94
 9   8   7   6   5   4   3   2   1

The sound of a slamming door echoed throughout the Martin household. Chris didn't care. In fact, he hoped it had been loud enough for the neighbors on the next block to hear. Or in the next town. He wanted everyone to know how really mad he was.

No, not mad. That wasn't . . . *violent* enough for what he felt. *Steamed. Ticked off. Hacked off.* . . . Several other terms ran through his mind, and he pictured his mom's face if he were to actually say them. A grim, somewhat satisfied smile crossed his face.

"Yeah, well, at least she can't tell me what to *think!*" he muttered fiercely. With a disgusted snort, Chris threw himself onto his bed, punching a pillow as he landed.

How could he have such a stick-in-the-mud mom? He snorted. Her reaction would have been understandable if he'd asked permission to go with the guys and rob a bank or do something really rotten. But to get upset about this? He could still see how she had squinted her eyes and frowned and her head had started to shake "no" before he'd finished his explanation.

"You know how I feel about those things, Chris," she'd said in that Mom voice she used any time she had to say something she was pretty sure he wouldn't like. She'd reached out to touch his arm and added, "It's your choice, but I'd really rather you didn't."

2

She didn't say you couldn't do what you wanted, a small voice in his head said.

"Yeah, right! Like I really have a choice."

I thought she was pretty reasonable about the whole thing—

"Whose side are you on?" Chris broke in with a disgusted snort. He knew if he thought about it for long, he'd stop being mad at his mom. After all, she was a pretty cool mom. She usually listened when Chris wanted to talk and treated him like someone who had brains instead of like some little moron. And she almost always tried to be fair. . . .

"Oh, no you don't!" he muttered fiercely. "I'm mad and I'm gonna stay mad. So you can just take your 'she's-a-pretty-good-mom' line and stuff it!"

With that, he jumped off the bed and paced the room. "I mean, what's so bad about reading some stupid books?" he said indignantly to the walls. "So what if they have horror stuff in 'em? It's not like it's real or anything. Does she think I'm gonna turn into some kind of psycho with a chain saw just because I read a book?" He stopped pacing and kicked his bed hard.

Too hard.

Pain shot through his foot and up his ankle. About the time it rounded his knee he had to grit his teeth to keep from screaming. "Man!" he said, plopping down on his bed. "I hope she's happy now. I'm probably crippled for life!"

Your mom didn't exactly make you kick the bed, that annoying voice remarked.

"Yeah, well, she made me mad, and if I wasn't mad I wouldn't have done something that stupid, so I guess it's as much her fault as anyone's."

Yeah, right. Like you never do stupid things all on your own—

"Oh, put a lid on it!" Chris snarled. He hated it when his conscience got sarcastic, especially since it was right so much of the time. And he had the nagging feeling that this was one of those times. The image of his mother's face when she'd seen the book he was reading flashed into his mind.

"Well, hey, it's not like I asked *her* to read it!" Sure, he'd known she wouldn't like those creepy books. In fact, she hated them. But was it his fault she didn't like good entertainment . . . ?

Good entertainment? the voice echoed (somewhat sarcastically, Chris thought).

"Yeah, good. I mean, the stories aren't the best, but they're OK. . . . And I don't really like all the gross and scary stuff, and the good guys usually get killed off. . . ." His voice trailed away. He was building more of a case for his mom's side than his own. Once again her image flitted into his mind, only this time what he saw was the look on her face as he'd yelled at her in frustration and then stormed out of the living room.

She looked pretty hurt, his conscience offered. Chris just stared across the room at his desk.

You really ought to apologize, it went on. *She only objects to something when she thinks it's important. And you didn't even give her a chance to explain.*

4

Chris stared at his desk even harder. That blasted conscience was starting to make sense again. If he could just find something to do, he could ignore it and go on with his day and enjoy being mad. If not . . . well, he'd probably end up feeling bad and tell his mom he was sorry and he loved her, and they'd hug and talk it all over.

Normally, that would have sounded like a good idea. But this time . . . well, there were just some things a kid had to stand firm on. Like whether or not he had the right to decide what he watched or read. Shoot, 95 percent of the kids at school read these books. The 5 percent that stayed away from that stuff were basically a bunch of chicken dweebs.

And if there was one thing Chris Martin wasn't, it was a chicken dweeb.

CHOICE ➡️

If Chris decides to apologize, turn to page 63.

If he sticks to his decision to stay angry, turn to page 132.

Chris clamped his teeth down before he said something angry. Unfortunately, he was just frustrated enough to be careless, and he chomped on his tongue.

Big time.

With a yelp of pain, he clutched his mouth and made all kinds of "I'm-in-pain!!" noises. To Jim, it just looked and sounded like Chris was doing a world-class imitation of a deranged gorilla . . . with the hiccups . . . doing the Watusi.

Suddenly Jim's anger was replaced by snorts, then snickers, then outright hoots of laughter.

"Blud are blue laghing ad?" Chris demanded, trying his best to communicate around a tongue that felt like it was a two-pound salami.

Jim just laughed even harder, leaning on his broom for support. In a few minutes, Chris was grinning, too.

"OK, tho maybe I thound a liddle funny," he snickered, and Jim went off again, laughing so hard he had to sit down on the floor. Chris just sat down, too, waiting for the guy to get a grip on himself.

"Whooo-eee," Jim finally said. "I'm sorry, Chris, but that was just too funny."

"I'm glad you found my pain so uplifting," he said with a sniff. But the grin on his face told his friend they were OK. "Now, what's the deal with the broom?"

Jim just grinned at him and handed him the broom.

6

"Hey, you said *whatever* I had in mind, you were up for it. Well, I promised Grandpa I'd clean the church for him today. I was calling to see if you wanted to do something after I was done, but when you offered your help, well, I never turn down a willing sucker!"

"Thanks a lot," Chris muttered. He got up and started to sweep as Jim pushed his way through the doors leading to the sanctuary. As the doors swung shut, Chris looked at what was one of his favorite features of the old church: the intricate lion and the beautiful lamb that were carved into the rich wood of the doors. Those carvings had always seemed sort of mysterious and regal to Chris. Right now, though, he could almost swear they were laughing at him.

"Oh well," he said with a sigh. "It beats taking out the garbage."

"And by the way," Jim added, poking his head through the doors again, "all the trash cans need to be emptied. I think there are about fifteen of them altogether, counting the ones in the classrooms and the offices. I'll let you do that while I vacuum in the sanctuary."

For the next half hour or so, Chris swept, dusted, emptied trash cans, and straightened papers until he thought he'd go crazy. Finally, though, the whole place looked great.

"All right!" Chris said with a grin. "We're outta here."

"Not quite," Jim said, and Chris shot him a suspicious look. "Don't worry," he said, patting his friend's arm. "I actually saved the best for last. We need to sweep out the bell tower, which I figured you wouldn't mind doing since it's one of your favorite places."

Chris followed his friend up the narrow staircase leading to the tower, then walked over to the window to look out. He loved how small the town looked from here, and how you could see treetops all around. The tower was such a great place! In fact, it would be perfect for . . .

Chris's eyebrows raised and a grin spread across his face. "Oh man, it's perfect! And I really am brilliant!"

Jim looked at his friend curiously. "This I gotta hear. You're brilliant? What brought you to that amazing conclusion?" Chris crossed over to him excitedly and grabbed his arm.

"The fact that I've just thought of something no one else has thought of."

"Such as?"

"Such as this place! It's perfect! Can't you just see it? You, me, the rest of the gang, here at night. Just us, no adults. And no lights, either! Just candles. And why would we all gather here in the dead of night? Simple, my dear Mr. Watson . . ."

Jim sighed and shook his head.

"We will be gathering for the world famous, annual 'Scariest Story in Existence' contest! Each one of us has to bring the scariest story he's ever heard and share it with the others!" Chris jumped around, clapping in glee. "We'll stay up all night, telling each other great stories. It'll be a blast!" His grin grew even wider as he looked at Jim.

"So? What do you think? Am I brilliant, or what?"

8

CHOICE ⇒

If Jim reacts positively to Chris's idea, turn to page 81.

If he's not so sure it's a great—or even a good—idea, turn to page 130.

Look, just because I'm a little late—"

"A *little* late?" Jim said. "I've been here for half an hour, cleaning this place by myself. I called you for some help, and you let me down!"

Chris knew he should just shut up, or apologize, or somehow try to calm things down. But on top of what he'd just gone through with his mom, this was too much.

"Listen, peanut brain," he stormed, "*if* I wanted to waste my time cleaning the church, which I sure don't, and *if* I thought you were going to be halfway fun to be around, which you sure aren't, and *if* you had the slightest bit of gratitude for my coming here to waste my time cleaning this church with you when you're such a royal pain in the neck, which you *don't,* I might stick around. But hey, I'm outta here!"

And he pushed his way out the door, leaving Jim standing there, trying to figure out just what exactly it was that Chris had just said. One thing was for sure, it had been an insult. And being insulted on top of being blown off was just too much.

Jim tightened his lips and went back to sweeping. It would be a long time before he called Chris for help again.

10

THE END

Some days it just seems as if blowing your top is all you can do. This must be that kind of day for Chris. But it didn't have to be that way. Turn to page 1 and see how the day could have gone if Chris had kept his cool.

Tina screamed. Suddenly a light was flashed on the doorway. Tina looked around and saw that Chris had seen the form, too, and he was directing the beam of his flashlight to reveal Rich standing there.

"Hey, kill the lights, kid!" he protested, laughing. Chris obliged with a sigh of relief. Rich came into the room and sat down next to Willy. "Sorry to scare you, but I was just listening to your stories."

The Ringers looked at each other uncomfortably. Would Rich tell Pastor Whitehead what they'd been doing?

"So, the whole point is to scare each other, eh?" Rich asked, and Chris nodded. A slow smile spread over the young man's face. "If you want to be scared, I've got a much better way to do it than a bunch of stories."

"What do you mean?" Sam asked, curious.

"Ever use a Ouija board?"

No one spoke, and Rich laughed again. "Come on, you guys. It's just a game! Don't look at me like I've just offered you some kind of snake!"

Tina and Jim looked at each other, doubt evident on their faces. They'd grown up in an environment much different from Millersburg. In Brazil, they'd seen a lot of things—spooky things, things involving spiritism and witchcraft—that just couldn't be explained away. Their parents had always been honest with them about the things that happened there, and about the ways in which God protected and worked through his followers.

"You never have to be afraid of the spirit world," Jim remembered his father saying. "God is within you, and he is more powerful than any evil spirit. But you shouldn't play with the spirit world, either. A lot of folks seem to think they can read about it and talk about it and even dabble in it without being touched. It just doesn't work that way. Satan is looking for any opening we give him to cause us, or others, unnecessary trouble. Walking into his camp just doesn't make sense."

His mother had added, "There are plenty of warnings in the Bible about avoiding witches and spiritists and things of the devil. God doesn't warn against things that don't matter." She had smiled and hugged them. "But I know I don't have to worry about you two. You're smart enough to know you need to stay away from those kinds of things."

Now as Jim looked at the interested faces of his friends, his parents' words seemed to ring in his ears.

"No," he said, "it's not just a game. And it's not something we should be playing with."

Rich looked at him, his eyebrows raised. "What's that supposed to mean?"

Jim felt his face getting hot with nervousness—what was he doing arguing with a guy who was going to be a minister? But he didn't back down. "I mean playing with Ouija boards isn't something I want to do."

"Oh, so you're afraid."

"I don't think it's a bad thing to be a little afraid of playing with the spirit world," Tina said.

"'The spirit world'? You make it sound like this has something to do with Satan!"

"Well—," Jim began, but Rich cut him off.

"And I bet you see a demon behind every bad thing that happens to someone, huh?" He sounded like he was talking to a particularly stupid little kid. Jim fought to hold on to his temper.

That became even more difficult when Willy leaned over and told Rich in an apologetic tone, "They're not as strange as they seem; they were just brought up in Brazil. This kind of stuff is more of a problem there."

"It's a problem everywhere, Willy," Jim said in a controlled voice. "And no, I don't think demons cause all the bad things that happen to us. But I do think they exist, and I think playing with something that has you supposedly calling on spirits to give you answers is foolish."

Rich shook his head. "You're way off, kid. All this thing does is hook up with what's inside of *you*. Any answers you're looking for are already there, inside of you, just waiting for you to bring them out. The Ouija is just a bridge to help you do that, to focus your mind and concentrate. It's all a mind thing, not a spirit thing."

His explanation sounded so . . . reasonable.

"So, what do the rest of you say?" Rich addressed the group. "You wanted something fun and scary, am I right? Well, this is it!"

14

CHOICE ⇒

If the Ringers side with Jim, turn to page 59.

If they decide to give the board a try, turn to page 37.

A few nights later, the whole gang had gathered at the church, armed with sleeping bags, pillows, bags of chips and cookies, five boxes of Bugles, and lots of pop. They talked excitedly as they climbed the stairs to the bell tower.

"This is great!" Jill said, going to look out one of the windows. "I can't believe we get to stay here overnight."

"Yeah, bats and all!" Sam said, winking at Chris and Pete.

Jill spun around. "Bats? What bats?"

"Oh, come on, Jill," Pete said, trying to sound serious. "Even you have to know that belfries have bats in them!"

"*Especially* you should know that!" Sam said. "Considering all the bats you've got in *your* belfry."

"Ha ha," Jill retorted. "You guys are a regular bunch of comedians."

"More like the Three Stooges if you ask me," Tina said.

"You wanna find bats?" Pete said. "I'll bet we'd find plenty of them over in the cemetery."

"Oh, now *there's* a great idea," Jill said. "Let's go roam around a cemetery at night, looking for bats. Why not just dig up one of the graves while you're at it?"

"Well, bats or no bats, I'm glad we get to stay here," Tina said. "I really didn't think Gramps would agree, but he said it was no problem as long as we stay at the church. He thought it sounded like so much fun he might even stop by later to join in."

Chris looked up sharply. "Did he mean that?"

Tina shrugged. "I don't know, probably not. I mean, he trusts us and everything." She stopped rolling out her sleeping bag and looked at Chris curiously. "Why?"

Chris smiled slightly. "Let's just say I've got some plans for tonight that will work out better if we're on our own."

"Plans?" Jill chimed in. "What plans? I thought we were just going to hang out here and talk and stuff."

Chris's grin grew wider. "Oh, we'll do that, and a lot more. In fact, Pete's idea isn't all that far off."

"I am *not* going on a bat hunt!" Jill said.

"And I'm not digging up any graves!" Sam added, a grimace on his face. "Not without heavy equipment!"

"No, no, it's neither one of those. But we *are* going on a hunt . . . and it *will* be in the cemetery."

Everyone was listening now.

"Come on, Chris, what are you talking about?" Willy asked.

"Yeah, no fair having secret plans," Pete agreed.

"Well-l-l-l . . ." Chris drew the word out until the others felt like it was four years long. "OK!" he said, then dug into his backpack and started spreading things out on his sleeping bag. The gang gathered around, then looked at each other curiously.

Chris had set out flashlights, whistles, several homemade maps, a couple of Instamatic cameras, and some squirt guns. He watched the confusion on his friends' faces with glee, then held up the newspaper clipping Jim had given him.

"*This* is our plan for the night," he announced dramatically. "We're going to catch the Midnight Marauder!"

"The midnight ma-who?"

"It's all here in the paper. Seems there's been a mysterious marauder wandering around the cemetery at night. People who live nearby have seen him . . . her . . . it, roaming around by the gravestones."

"So what?" Jill asked, still confused.

Jim answered her. "It's against the law to be in the cemetery after hours. I guess the caretakers are afraid people might vandalize the older gravestones. Did you know that some of them are a hundred years old? Anyway, every time the police get a report and show up, there's no one around."

"Listen up," Chris said, then read the article out loud. It told how one elderly woman who lived across the street from the cemetery had said it was as though the marauder "just vanished into thin air" whenever the police cars pulled up.

When Chris stopped reading and looked around, he saw interest and anticipation in all the eyes around him. All, that is, except for Tina's eyes. There was no anticipation there. Instead, there was dismay.

"This cemetery is just down the street from here," Chris said triumphantly. "So I figured this would be the perfect opportunity for us to go and see if we can catch this guy."

18

Sam was looking at their gear. "OK, so I get the flashlights and the maps. But what are the whistles for?"

"To use if we get into trouble," Chris said. "One blast on a whistle and we'll all come running."

"What about the squirt guns?" Willy asked, peering over Pete's shoulder.

A smug look crossed Chris's face. "Those, my dear Watson, are the perfect tool for catching our man." He reached out to pick one up. "I've filled them with India ink. When you see the marauder, you give him a couple of squirts, and *voilà*, he's marked but good!"

"Ink washes off, Mr. Genius," Sam remarked, unimpressed. But Chris shook his head.

"Not this ink. Once it's on your hands or clothes, it's there until it wears off." He looked around and grinned. "So, any ideas who or what this mystery marauder might be?"

"Maybe there's more than one," Jill suggested, and the Ringers were off, everyone chiming in with possibilities. Everyone but Tina. She just listened to the suggestions: a crook up to no good, a runaway hiding out, gang members doing drug transactions, kids messing around. . . .

Finally she couldn't take it anymore. "But we'd have to go to the cemetery to catch this guy," she broke in. Jim rolled his eyes.

"That's what I like about you, Sis," he said sarcastically. "Your keen sense of the obvious."

She pinned Jim with her eyes. "Gramps said we weren't supposed to leave the church, remember?"

He shifted uncomfortably. "Well, yeah, but this isn't like we're going out to cause trouble."

"Right!" Chris was obviously in full agreement. "We're trying to help the police. Pastor Whitehead wouldn't object to that."

"Besides," Sam piped up, "how dangerous could it be to walk around a cemetery at night? I mean, the only people we would bother aren't exactly going to complain!"

Tina shook her head, unconvinced. Everyone else seemed to think this was a great idea—and it *did* sound like a real adventure. But she didn't feel right about it, and she was pretty sure there would be one other person who wouldn't think it was right: her grandfather.

Biting her lip, she stared down at the stuff on Chris's bag, wondering what to do.

CHOICE ⇔

If Tina refuses to go on the Marauder Hunt, turn to page 69.

If she decides it's OK, turn to page 105.

Jill was so frightened that she clenched her eyes shut, and a tear slipped down her cheek. She hated being afraid!

Suddenly she wasn't afraid anymore. No, she'd gone way past that. Now she was terrified . . . pure, unadulterated, spine-melting, knee-quivering terror washed over every inch of her as she wondered frantically what to do.

I will not be afraid. . . .

She frowned. Had that been a voice?

I will not be afraid, for you are close. . . .

No, not a voice, but a memory—a memory that suddenly came to her with startling clarity. She could see her mother reaching out to hold her after Jill had had a nightmare one night when she was young. And she could hear her mother's voice as she recited one of her favorite Bible verses: "Even when walking through the dark valley of death I will not be afraid, for you are close beside me, guarding, guiding all the way."

Jill opened her eyes and smiled. She wasn't alone; God was with her. And he would take care of her.

"I forgot, God," she whispered to herself, "but just for a minute." The panic subsided, and she felt herself start to relax. Listening carefully, she heard nothing but silence. Whatever—whoever—had been there seemed to be gone. She stood up and stepped forward cautiously—and felt her foot hit something. Looking down, she saw the moonlight reflect off of something silver.

Her flashlight! Her smile widened to a grin, and she reached down to grab it and turn it on. Flashing the comforting beam around her, she gave a yelp of triumph as she spotted her whistle too.

Grabbing it up, she gave a loud, long blast, then settled back.

She didn't know if what she'd heard had been the marauder. Maybe it had, maybe it hadn't. The others might be upset when they reached her because she'd whistled without actually catching the marauder. But Jill didn't care because she'd realized something.

She shouldn't be there, and neither should any of the others. She intended to tell them that when they got there. They could listen, and they could agree or disagree. Either way, when she finished talking to them she was going to go back to the church, accompanied by whoever cared to come.

She was finished with this adventure.

THE END

Not ready to give up on the marauder yet? Turn to page 15, or page 105 for more crazy adventures!

Tina made up her mind.

"Gramps, did anyone tell you what we're going to do at the church?" she asked.

"No, not that I can recall."

"Well, we're . . . that is, Chris and Jim . . . ," she faltered and stopped. It was no use. As much as she wanted to tell him, she just couldn't be a tattletale.

"What's wrong, Tina?" her grandfather asked, his eyes twinkling. "You Ringers planning to paint the church purple or something?"

Tina grinned weakly. "No, nothing like that. We're just going to have a storytelling contest, that's all."

"Oh, well that should be a lot of fun," Pastor Whitehead said with a smile. "In fact, I can remember sitting around the campfire with my family when I was a kid and everyone telling stories."

Tina's eyes widened. "You did? What kind of stories?"

"Oh, mostly ghost stories," he remarked, making Tina's eyes grow even wider.

"Ghost stories?!" she squeaked. "You?"

He grinned at her. "Well, I *was* a kid, Tina. And kids are always interested in things that are scary and spooky. It's just a part of being young."

"So you don't think telling scary stories is a bad thing?" she asked.

He was silent for a moment, then answered her slowly. "Well now, I wouldn't say that. I guess it depends on the kind of stories. The stories we told were pretty harmless," he grinned crookedly. "Actually, they were kind of silly. By kids' standards today, they probably wouldn't even raise an eyebrow. And that's the problem."

Tina frowned. "I don't understand."

"There are a lot more scary things in today's world, what with the kinds of books and movies that are out now. And they all seem to go beyond just giving people a good scare. They seem to rely pretty heavily on the occult or on the power of evil. I think when people use those things they're playing with something they just don't understand. And I don't think telling—or watching or reading—those kinds of stories is a very good idea."

"I don't think so either," Tina said with determination. Suddenly she knew what she had to do. "Um, Gramps, would you excuse me? I need to go talk to someone." Almost before he had a chance to respond, she jumped up and ran out of the room.

Pastor Whitehead smiled to himself as he settled back against the cushions of the couch. Something was going on, and he had the distinct feeling that this little talk had just put something in motion. He didn't know what, but that was OK. He trusted God to watch out for his grandchildren—and for the other Ringers.

He closed his eyes and prayed for them.

"Jim, we have to talk. Now."

Jim looked up in surprise at the serious tone in Tina's voice. He was even more surprised to see that Chris, Jill,

Sam, and Willy were with her. They came into his room and plopped down on the bed.

"What's this all about?" he asked Chris, who just shrugged.

"Got me. Princess Tina here called us all and told us to get ourselves over here pronto. She said she had something important to tell us."

"OK, Princess," Willy said, picking up on Chris's name for Tina. "We're here, so what's up?"

Tina paused. *Oh, help, God!* she prayed quickly. *Help me say this right.* Then she said firmly, "Here's the deal. I want to know how many of us really want to tell scary stories at the overnighter."

Silence met her question for a second or two, as everyone looked at each other. Tina bit her lip nervously.

CHOICE ⇒

If someone really wants to tell spooky stories, turn to page 134.

If no one really cares, turn to page 71.

If the vote is split, turn to page 33.

Tina stared at her clock. Nine o'clock. She wondered what the gang was doing right now. She sighed.

It had been hard to tell the others she wasn't going to the overnight. Jim had even gotten kind of mad at her.

"You just want to act like you're better than the rest of us," Jim had said.

"You don't think this overnight is such a hot idea either!" she'd shot back. "But you're too afraid to say no!"

"*I'm* afraid? *I'm* not the one who's staying home!"

"Right. And you know why you're not?" He started to answer, but she cut him off. "I'll tell you why! 'Cause you're afraid Chris or Sam or one of the others will call you chicken! But that's what you are! You're a big chicken who's too afraid to say no to something you know is wrong!"

As if their fight wasn't bad enough, Chris and Jill had called her to find out why she wasn't going. When she tried to explain, they both had gotten frustrated with her. Chris had argued, like Jim, that they were just going to have fun and that she was being a stick-in-the-mud. Jill's argument was a little different, but no less hurtful.

"We girls are supposed to stick together, Tina, remember? We're not supposed to just blow each other off like this. If you don't come, it'll just be me and all the boys.

And that's no fun. At least it's not as much fun as when you and I are there together."

Tina had tried to explain, but it hadn't helped. Jill just got more frustrated and ended the call with "OK. Fine. You do what you *think* you have to do. But don't blame me when you realize all the fun you miss out on, Miss I'm-Doing-the-Right-Thing."

Things had gone downhill from there. When Chris came by to get Jim, neither one of them was speaking to her. And she knew it would take awhile before Jill cooled down.

Tears smarted Tina's eyes, and she rubbed her fists against them. Sometimes doing what you believed was right didn't feel very good. In fact, right now it felt downright lousy—and lonely. Really, really lonely.

"This just isn't fair!" she said fiercely. She went to flop on her bed. "All I wanted to do was the right thing. . . ." Her words trailed off as she remembered how she'd snapped at Jim, whined at Chris, and argued with Jill. Suddenly, as she stared at her ceiling, she felt pretty bad about the way she'd acted. It was OK that she'd decided not to go to the overnight. And it was OK to think the gang's plans weren't a great idea. But it definitely *wasn't* OK to get mean with her brother and friends.

She turned over and buried her face in her pillow. *What a mess!* she thought in frustration. *Now the whole night is wasted!*

Or was it?

She paused, then sat up. Maybe there was still something she could do. Frowning in thought, she reached for her Bible where it lay on her nightstand. Quickly she thumbed through the pages until she found the section she wanted. Ah, there it was: James 5:13, 16.

> Is any one of you in trouble? He should pray. . . . The prayer of a righteous man is powerful and effective.

She set her Bible down with a thoughtful look on her face. Yep, she was in trouble all right. No doubt about it. When your brother *and* your friends all thought you were a jerk, you were definitely in trouble.

But she might not be the only one. If Jim and the others were doing something God wouldn't like, they might be in trouble, too.

Is any one of you in trouble? He should pray. . . .

Maybe tonight didn't have to be a waste after all.

Tina hugged her knees and started to pray. "Lord," she whispered, "I'm sorry I was so mean to Jim today. Please forgive me. And help him to forgive me too. I was just mad. And I'm sorry about getting mad at Chris and Jill and feeling sorry for myself. Help us to work things out, Lord. They're my friends, and I don't want us to be mad at each other. And Lord, if you'd be with the Ringers at the church, that'd be really great. Protect them, and help them not to do or say anything you wouldn't like. And if telling these stories is a bad idea, then, please, tell them so. Thanks, God. Amen."

A good feeling swept over Tina as she finished praying. It felt a lot like when her mom or dad hugged her and told her they were proud of her. And that feeling stayed

28

with her the rest of the evening. And later, as she turned off the light and snuggled under her covers, there was a smile on her face.

She wasn't sure whether or not her prayer had helped her brother and her friends, but she was sure of one thing: It sure had helped her!

THE END

Don't stop reading! You'll miss the Ringers' moonlight mystery at the cemetery, and the blowup in the bell tower, and the attack of the Midnight Marauder, and . . . oh, lots of things that you won't want to miss. So go back to page 139 and see where the other choices lead.

Think about the *Nightmare* movies, Chris. Doesn't the killer keep coming back to life, no matter what the good guys do? Isn't that why the movies are still going?"

Chris thought about that for a minute, then nodded. "Yeah, I guess you're right." He frowned. "But the good guys have to win eventually, don't they?"

Mrs. Martin smiled. "Well, you and I know they do, because of what the Bible tells us." Chris nodded. He and his mom had talked a lot about what people called the end times, when the whole world was just supposed to go up in smoke. He'd been kind of nervous about it all, especially when he read in the Bible that there would be earthquakes and floods and fires and lots of people getting hurt when the end of the world came. But his mom had helped him see that, no matter what happens to people here, if they are Christians they don't need to be afraid. Because in the end, they will stand on the winning side with God and Christ. And when this world is over with, it will only be the beginning—of eternity—for God's family.

"Unfortunately," Mrs. Martin continued, "movies like the Nightmare series, and a lot of those kinds of books and TV movies, make it look like evil is a lot stronger than good. They show at least some of the good people getting killed or hurt. And while the evil may be stopped for a while, it isn't ever totally stopped."

Chris looked at his mom in surprise. "How do you know that, Mom? I mean, you haven't read these books or seen one of these movies . . ." His eyes widened in shock. *"Have you?"*

She grinned at him. "As a matter of fact, I have."

"What?!" Chris almost fell off his chair.

Laughing, his mom explained. "Remember last fall when I told you my parents' group at the church was having movie nights for a week or two?"

"Well, sure, but I figured you guys were watching some Disney movies or some goopy love stories or some of those Christian movies. . . . I never figured you guys were watching Freddy Kreuger! I mean, you get grossed out by the stuff stuck in the garbage disposal!"

His mom nodded, smiling wryly. "I know, and it wasn't a lot of fun. But several of us were concerned about these books and movies, and about how much our kids seem to like them. So we talked to Pastor Whitehead about it, and we all decided to rent one of the movies and watch it together. Afterward, we had a discussion time about what we saw. Then we all bought a couple of the more popular horror books and read them, highlighting the things that bothered or concerned us. And I'll tell you something, Chris, there were more than just a few places that I highlighted. By the time we were finished, I didn't like the messages I got from any of these horror books or movies."

"Like the evil never dying?"

"That, and the message that death is an escape, and that life is cheap, and that evil is power—"

"OK, OK," Chris said, his hands up in surrender. "I get

the point. So you don't want me getting into this stuff because it all has a bad message?"

She smiled. "I don't know that it all does, but a lot of it seems to. But there's something more. They aren't the kind of books or movies you can forget easily," she added quietly.

Chris looked at her curiously. "What do you mean?"

She sighed. "As much as I'd like to, I can't get some of those images out of my mind," she said. "I've even had some nightmares because of what I read and saw. But I figured the time would come when you'd be curious about these things, and I wanted to know what I was talking about when I said no." She smiled.

Chris shook his head. "I'm sorry you had to watch something like that because of me, Mom."

She touched his face and smiled. "It's OK, Chris. You and your sister are the most important people in my life. I'll do whatever I have to to take care of you. And God is helping me get past the nightmares and the fears those things stirred up. So don't worry about me."

Chris sat looking at his mom in amazement. He could hardly believe she'd done all of that just for him and his sister. *I'm one lucky guy to have such a cool mom,* he thought. He leaned forward and hugged her. "OK, so no horror movies or books or shows. But how about this for an alternate plan? We find a movie we all can watch—"

"Even Nancy?" his mom asked. She was well aware that Chris usually did everything he could to avoid spending time with his nine-year-old sister.

"Sure, even Nancy." (Hey, he was feeling pretty good right now. So he could afford to be generous and grant her

32

some time in his presence.) He wiggled his eyebrows at his mom. "And *then* we get pizza and stop at the Freeze for sundaes for dessert!"

She laughed and hugged him back. "Sounds like a great time. But right now," she said, giving him a push toward the door, "Jim is still waiting for you."

"Oh no!" Chris said, "I forgot!"

He raced out of the house, jumped on his bike, and made record time getting to the church. Dashing up the stairs, he pulled open the heavy wooden doors and burst inside, startling Jim, who rounded on him angrily.

"Well, well, look who's here. Mr. I'll-Be-Right-There," he said, his voice heavy with sarcasm.

Chris stopped in his tracks, an angry response jumping to his mind.

If Chris responds angrily, turn to page 9.

If he stops himself, turn to page 5.

I want to," Chris said. He looked at Sam and Jim pointedly, raising his eyebrows as if to say "Well?"

"Yeah, me too," they said almost together.

"Well, *I* don't," Jill said, a stubborn look settling on her face. "And I think it's a really stupid idea!"

"I suppose you can think of something better?" Chris demanded.

"Get a life!" she retorted. "A warthog could think of something better."

"Ah, but a warthog would have difficulty communicating his ideas," said Sam. Chris gave him an annoyed look and then glared back at Jill.

"You should know," Chris said sweetly. "You look enough like a warthog to be able to speak for one." Sam and Jim burst into laughter, and Jill reddened at the insult.

"Nice mouth, Chris," she said coldly.

"Hey, Jill," Tina said uncomfortably, desperately trying to calm things down. "You did kind of start it, you know?"

Suddenly Jill turned on her furiously. "What? *I* started it? I'm not the one who called this stupid meeting!"

"Nice mouth, Jill," Chris mocked her in a singsong voice.

Suddenly there was a loud bang, and everyone jumped in shock. Everyone, that is, except Tina, who was standing next to the door she'd just slammed as hard as she could. The others stared at her in amazement.

"There, that's better," she said at their silence. "Now, if you're all finished insulting each other, how about we just start this little meeting over?"

Jill started to say something, but Tina held up her hand. Compressing her lips, Jill sank down onto a chair.

"All in favor of the scary stories, raise your hand," Tina commanded. The four guys raised their hands. "All against?" she said, and she and Jill raised their hands.

"How about a compromise?" Chris asked.

"What do you mean?" Jill said.

"You and Tina can have your own overnighter here, or at your house. Then you can do whatever you want. Us guys can go to the church and have our scary story overnighter."

"Yeah, but it's being in the bell tower that makes the overnighter fun," Tina said.

"Well, then we'll just have another overnighter before the summer's over," Sam proposed. "And we won't tell stories at that one."

Jill and Tina looked at each other.

"What do you think?" Tina asked.

CHOICE ⇒

Do the girls agree to the compromise? Turn to page 125.

Do they decide the guys are just trying to have all the fun without them? Turn to page 41.

Chris lost it. He snickered. Then he laughed. Long and loud, for several minutes.

Jim tried to stay angry, but the sight of Chris snorting and hooting and holding his sides finally got to him, and he started to grin.

"Hoo boy," Chris managed to say between hoots, "you looked just like a massive hulk about to take apart some goon. That was great! You should be in the movies!"

Jim shook his head and punched Chris playfully on the arm. "Yeah, well, you deserved getting taken apart. You've been a real putz since you got to the church, you know?"

Chris wiped tears from his eyes and nodded. "Yeah, I know. This has been one rotten day so far." He looked at Jim sheepishly. "Sorry for getting so mad. I just lost it there for a minute."

"Yeah, me too. I'm sorry I acted like a jerk and wouldn't tell you about the marauder." He grinned. "It's just that I'm usually the one who doesn't know what's going on, so it was kind of fun to be on the other end for a change."

They turned and went back into the church. "OK, so what *is* the story about this marauder guy?" Chris asked.

Jim went to his jacket and pulled out a newspaper clipping. Chris read it through, then his face lit up with excitement and he slapped Jim on the back. "Way to go, Jim ol' boy!" he said gleefully. "This is definitely a job for the Ringers! And I know just when and where to talk to them about it."

Turn to page 15.

Come on, Jim," Willy said. "Rich is studying to be a minister. He should know if something is wrong or dangerous."

"Exactly!" Rich said. But Tina shook her head.

"No way," she said. "I'm not playing with a Ouija. And I'll guarantee you my grandfather wouldn't be too happy to know we'd done so, either!"

At that, Rich fixed her with a cold stare. "What are you, his little informer?"

"Hey, chill," Chris said defensively, looking at Rich. "You don't need to talk to her that way. She's just saying what she thinks."

"Yeah, well, if you ask me, she thinks all wrong. Besides, she's just a dumb little girl who's scared of the dark. Didn't I hear you say something along those lines?" He was looking at Chris now, and something in his eyes made Chris really uncomfortable.

It was as though there was more at stake than just playing some game. Surprised, Chris looked at Jim, who raised his eyebrows as though to say "See what I mean? This just isn't cool." Chris nodded and turned back to Rich.

"Yeah, I said that," he admitted. "And I was wrong to do so. I should have known better than to insult a friend. But then, I wouldn't expect you to know that because you're not our friend."

Rich started to speak, but Chris kept going.

"Now Jim here, *he's* definitely our friend. He knows us, and we know him. So I guess it's kind of stupid for us to take your word over his, isn't it? I mean, seeing as we don't really know you and all."

Rich looked around at the gang and saw nothing but polite—and resistant—expressions. He shook his head.

"I thought you guys wanted to have some fun," he said, trying one last time.

"We do," Jill said. "But what we were doing—and what you wanted us to do—isn't having fun. It's playing with something we shouldn't be playing with."

"And who told you that?" Rich challenged.

Jill smiled. "Actually, you did." At the stunned look on Rich's face, her smile grew broader. "You were so determined to get us to play your Ouija board that you crossed a real important line. You were unkind and insulting. We don't do that to each other here—" She broke off and looked at Tina apologetically. "Well, not usually anyway. When what we're doing starts to matter more than our friends and how we treat them, then something's wrong."

"So thanks, but no thanks," Willy concluded.

"Yeah, bucko," Sam agreed.

Rich rose and walked to the doorway. "You guys don't know what you're missing," he said.

"Maybe not," Jim responded. "But I'm not going to worry about missing out on something that God doesn't want me to do anyway."

With a snort, Rich walked out of the room and went down the stairs.

Nobody said anything for a minute, then the room came alive. Chris and Jill went over to Tina to apologize for being mean to her. Sam and Willy went to slap Jim on the back and tell him how great he'd been while talking with Rich. Everyone was filled with a sense of relief, as though they'd just been through some kind of test and passed—barely.

"I can't believe someone studying to be a minister would think that stuff is OK," Willy said later on.

Jim shrugged. "I guess even people who want to be ministers can be deceived."

"That's why we need each other," Chris added. "So we can let each other know when we're off the mark." A sheepish expression crossed his face. "Like I was about this monster story contest. I'm sorry, you guys, for being such a pain. I don't even know anymore why I thought it sounded like so much fun."

"We were thinking maybe you ate a bad tamale or something," joked Willy.

"Yeah, but that's OK, Chris," Sam said. "If you weren't a pain at least once a week, we wouldn't know what to do with you."

"I'll tell you one thing," Jim added. "I'm going to talk to my grandfather about this guy and what he said."

"That's a good idea." Sam nodded. "I'd like to listen in, too, so I can hear what Pastor Whitehead has to say about this spirit world stuff."

"So let's have a group discussion," Jill jumped in. "In

fact, we could call him now and see if he can come over. I'm not so sure I want to spend the rest of the evening with Mr. Charm School as our chaperon."

"Great idea," Willy said.

And so they called Pastor Whitehead, who showed up a few minutes later, relieved Rich of his responsibilities, and spent the rest of the evening talking, praying, and laughing with the Ringers.

THE END

Don't stop now! There are still adventures to be discovered. Turn back to the beginning and explore another story!

I think you guys are just trying to cut us out of the fun," Jill said, her eyes stormy.

"Aw, Jill—," Chris began, but he didn't get far. Jill jumped out of her chair, stomped to the door, and pulled it open. She turned back for a second, and the others were surprised to see tears in her eyes.

"I think it's really rotten to invite me to something fun, then make it so I can't go," she said, her voice tight. "So you just go ahead and have your stupid story contest. It's pretty clear you care more about that than you do about whether or not Tina and I come!"

With that, she stormed out of the room. The others sat there, looking at each other or at the floor.

"OK, so . . . I guess that settles it," Tina said, sounding like she was about to cry.

"Hey, Sis, don't let it get to you. Jill's just mad. She'll get over it," Jim said. Tina turned on him, her hands clenched into fists.

"Maybe she will, and maybe she won't. But I think she's right about you caring more about your stupid contest than you do about us."

Before Jim could answer, she was gone. They could hear her running down the hall to her own room.

Chris cleared his throat. "Um . . . I guess the stories

aren't that big of a deal," he said. The hurt look in Jill's eyes had made him feel pretty crummy.

"Yeah," Jim agreed. "I mean, if it means the girls won't come, then it's kind of bad. It's just more fun when they're along." He glanced at Sam, who just shrugged as if to say "Whatever you guys want to do is OK with me."

"Right. OK," Chris said. "No scary stories." He was quiet for a few seconds, then cleared his throat again. "So, who wants to go tell the girls?"

No one moved.

"Maybe we should just leave them alone for a while," Sam suggested. Chris and Jim nodded, all too willing to do just that.

"So, what have you got around here to eat?" Willy asked Jim. The four of them headed for the kitchen to rummage through the fridge. But as they did so, Chris wondered if Tina and Jill would even be interested in the overnighter anymore. He sure hoped so, because, now that he thought about it, he knew that things *weren't* nearly as much fun without the whole gang there.

THE END

Turn to page 142.

Taking a deep breath, Jill forced the panic away. "Relax," she told herself, glancing around. The only light came from the full moon that shone down on her.

Well, as long as the moon stays out, I can see well enough to find someone, she thought. She stood up and started to walk.

"Willy?" she whispered again loudly, trying to keep her voice from shaking. "P-Pete . . . ?"

There was no answer. Only the wind rustling the leaves in the trees around her. She bit her lip, fighting against the panic that again threatened to overwhelm her. She knew the others had to be close by. But that thought offered her little comfort, for suddenly all the ghost and monster stories she'd ever heard danced through her mind, growing more and more frightening with every minute. She looked around again, sure that every gravestone hid a terrible fiend, and that someone—or some*thing*—was just waiting to grab her as she walked by.

Jill heard a sound . . . a rustling that seemed to be coming from somewhere nearby. She froze and peered into the darkness. She couldn't see anything, but she could definitely hear something.

There was someone—some*thing*—there!

44

CHOICE ⇥

If Jill tries to stay calm and find her flashlight, turn to page 20.

If she gives in to her fears, turn to page 54.

Chris watched as Pastor Whitehead moved away. How could he just leave like that without finding out who the marauder was?

Setting his jaw stubbornly, Chris turned to move closer to the cemetery. He wanted a better look at this guy. But as he took a step, his foot landed on a brittle branch. The loud *snap* was almost deafening in the quiet of the night.

The man spun around. "Who's there?" he demanded.

Chris looked at Pastor Whitehead—who had stopped and turned back toward him—ready for any sign that they should run. But instead, Pastor Whitehead just shook his head and walked out from the cover of the tree. Startled, Chris followed.

"There's no need to be alarmed," Mr. Whitehead said. "We're from the Capitol Community Church, and we just want to talk."

Chris followed Pastor Whitehead as he slowly walked toward the man, stepped over the waist-high iron fence, and came into the light of a small campfire—wondering all the way if the pastor had suddenly gone totally nuts! *God, please keep us safe!* he prayed. This wasn't some helpless old guy standing there, peering at them in the firelight. It was the Midnight Marauder! The Vanishing Villain! The Mystery Man of All Time! The—

Chris's thoughts stopped abruptly. In the firelight, he could see the marauder clearly, and he swallowed uncomfortably. He wasn't an old man, but he wasn't young either. Chris couldn't tell exactly how old he was because his face was almost covered by long scraggly hair and a mess of a beard. The guy's clothes looked as though they hadn't seen the inside of a washing machine in days . . . weeks . . . *years,* and Chris could see that his dirty hands were trembling as they clutched and unclutched his ragged shirt front.

This guy was no marauder! He was pitiful!

Pastor Whitehead stepped forward, extending his hand. "Leonard Whitehead," he said, introducing himself. "I'm the pastor at Capitol Community Church. This is Chris, one of my friends from the church."

After a pause, the man took the pastor's hand and shook it briefly. "Adams. Joshua Adams." His voice was low and gravelly, as though it were rusty from not being used. Chris noted how his eyes kept darting to look behind them in the darkness.

"Don't worry," Pastor Whitehead said, "the police aren't with us."

The man's eyes shot back to the pastor's face, then fell to the ground. Chris watched him, shifting uncomfortably. *He looks like he's ashamed of something,* he thought and glanced around at the man's camp. There was a thin blanket laid out on the ground and a can of something— Chris wrinkled his nose—something he wouldn't care to eat, cooking on the edge of the fire.

"You gonna call the cops?" Adams asked in a low voice. Pastor Whitehead met his eyes.

"We already have. They're going to meet us at the cemetery entrance." The man chewed at his lip nervously, but Pastor Whitehead seemed calm and unworried. "You know we have to tell them about you." The man nodded shortly. "But you don't have to go to jail," Pastor Whitehead continued.

The man eyed the pastor suspiciously. "Vagrancy's illegal," he said, "I know that, and I expect to pay the penalty if I'm caught."

Chris was surprised at the way Mr. Adams sounded almost, well, *dignified* when he said that. He shook his head. How did someone end up living like this?

"You think I'm some kind of bum, don't you, kid? That I live this way 'cause I want to, or 'cause I'm lazy?"

The questions startled Chris and he looked away, embarrassed. How could he admit that that was exactly what he had been thinking?

"Look at you," Adams went on, his tone heavy with sarcasm, nodding his head toward Chris's Lazer Tag gear. "Fancy-schmancy toys, nice new clothes, expensive tennis shoes . . . you think you're too good to even look at trash like me."

"That's not true!" Chris retorted, meeting the man's hard gaze defiantly.

"No?"

"No." Chris's response was quiet, but firm. There was a pause as Joshua Adams held Chris's eyes, daring him to look away. He didn't. Finally, Chris thought he saw a slight smile cross the man's grungy face.

"Maybe not, maybe not," he muttered. Then, looking around his camp with a sigh, he turned back to Pastor Whitehead. "Been a good place to live. Nice and quiet. No one coming by to tell me to get lost or get a job." He laughed a short, bitter laugh. "Like it's so easy."

"It's not, is it," Pastor Whitehead agreed, and the man shook his head.

"Been trying for over a year . . ." His voice trailed off and he looked at his hands. "I'm a carpenter, you know? A carpenter! I'm not some bum who doesn't have any skills to offer!" That short, hard laugh came again. "But if you don't have a 'permanent residence,' nobody wants you." A trace of anger crossed the man's tired face. "So tell me, how am I supposed to get a permanent residence without a job?" He looked around at the gravestones. "Guess I'll just have to join these folks here, huh? At least no one's going to chase them off."

Chris felt bad for the man and looked at Pastor Whitehead. He was watching the guy, just listening and nodding. Finally, he said, "Mr. Adams, if you'll come with me to talk to the police, I'll do what I can to help you."

"Yeah, right. I been 'helped' by churches before," he said coldly. "They give you a buck or two, an encouraging pat on the back, and a fine see-you-later. Some help."

"Pastor Whitehead isn't like that! He really cares about people, and you'd see that if you'd just stop being so angry and give him a chance!" Chris retorted. Who did this guy think he was to talk to the pastor that way?

Pastor Whitehead put his hand on Chris's shoulder and squeezed slightly. "It's OK, Chris. Mr. Adams has every right to refuse our help." He paused and met the man's eyes. "But I hope he won't."

There was silence for a few seconds, then the Midnight Marauder sighed and stuck his hands in his pockets. "OK, Pastor, let's go see the boys in blue."

Chris wanted to cheer, but he managed to keep his mouth shut. He wasn't sure Pastor Whitehead would be able to help Mr. Adams . . . but he knew someone who could. And, as they headed for the cemetery entrance, he offered another prayer, this time asking the Lord to help the ragged man walking beside them to find a job, and a home—and something, somewhere, to make him not feel so alone.

THE END

Turn to page 142.

Mom," he said, trying to be patient. "Jim is waiting for me."

He could tell she was trying to be reasonable about the whole thing by the way she paused, like she was taking a deep breath to calm down.

"Where are you meeting Jim?" she asked.

"At the church, like I already said."

"What are you boys going to do?" she asked.

A wave of frustration washed over him. "Come on, Mom!" he exploded, the words coming out in a rush of anger. "All I want to do is go out for a little while. I mean, you tell me what I can and can't read or watch. Can't I have a *little* freedom? Or do you have to know everything I'm going to do? I just don't feel like talking now, OK?"

His mom's eyes flashed then, and Chris felt his face burn. But he wasn't going to back down! She'd probably order him to go back to his room—and he'd go, but he'd stomp all the way until he shook the apartment. He stared at her defiantly, waiting, but she just sighed and stood silent for a beat.

Then she nodded. "OK, Chris, if that's how you want to do this, we'll wait," she said with a voice that was low and controlled. Then she looked him square in the eyes, and he felt his face burn at the frustration and disappointment he read there. "But when you get home, and I would prefer that you did so before suppertime, we *are* going to talk."

Chris nodded shortly, then went out the door. He got his bike from the garage and started down the road. He should feel good, free—after all, he'd won this round. But a strange heaviness had settled in his chest. He and his mom didn't fight often, especially not like they had today. And especially not over something like a stupid book.

He felt his face burn as he remembered the way he'd yelled at her. Suddenly there were tears stinging his eyes.

If I was smart, I'd turn around and go talk to her. But he didn't. He just kept pedaling, feeling rotten, wishing he'd never mentioned the book or that he could start that whole stupid day over again.

THE END

Chris can't start his day over, but you can! Just turn to page 63 and see what happens.

Chris spun around and ran back to the clearing. Pastor Whitehead hadn't blown the whistle yet, so he and Sam would still be at the clearing.

Sure enough, they were there, Pastor Whitehead counting out loud. Chris came running up to them and grabbed Pastor Whitehead's arm, gasping for breath.

"Chris!" Pastor Whitehead said, startled. "What's wrong?"

"Marauder . . . there . . . gotta . . . catch . . . !" he gasped, but Pastor Whitehead just shook his head.

"I'm sorry, Chris, I don't understand."

"I think he's trying to say he saw the Midnight Marauder!" Jim said from behind them. He had spotted Chris running toward the clearing and decided something was up. Quickly, Jim explained to his grandfather about the story in the newspaper. Pastor Whitehead looked at the three boys speculatively.

"Would this marauder have anything to do with the little adventure you didn't want to explain to me earlier?" he asked, and Jim and Chris felt their faces turn red.

"Well, sort of . . . ," Chris said. "But not really, since we decided against the adventure."

Pastor Whitehead's eyebrows raised slightly. "Good decision," he said, then turned to Jim. "Run back to the church, Jim, and call the police. Tell them to meet us at the entrance to the cemetery. We'll round up the others, then I'll go with Chris to see if we can find out who—"

"Or what!" Sam broke in, but Pastor Whitehead just ignored him.

"*Who* Chris saw in the cemetery," he finished. Jim headed for the church as Pastor Whitehead lifted his whistle and gave a series of short blasts. He looked at Chris and Sam. "Well, here's hoping they understand they need to come back here, even though the game hasn't started yet."

CHOICE

If the Ringers return to the clearing, turn to page 128.

If some of them return, but some think it's a trick to make them reveal their hiding places, turn to page 137.

Jill couldn't take it anymore. She drew herself up, gulped a chestful of air, and screamed at the top of her lungs.

Suddenly, just as Jill got halfway through her breath, someone—some*thing*—grabbed her arm and held it in a steely grip.

Jill did the only thing any intelligent person would do: She frantically tried to jerk away, screaming again and again. But whatever had hold of her wouldn't let go, and a grimy hand came up to grab her shirt collar and shake her fiercely.

She could hear a low voice rumbling at her, but she was so terrified the words made no sense. She struck out with her hands and feet, fighting for all she was worth. The darkness hid her attacker's face—but that didn't matter, because she had her eyes closed anyway. She didn't want to see who—or what—had her. She just wanted to get away.

Then, just as suddenly as she had been grabbed, she was free. And she went sprawling on the ground with a thud. She heard yelling and what sounded like a scuffle and opened her eyes.

Beams of light flashed all around her and two forms were coming right at her.

"Jill! Jill! Are you OK?"

She stared in mute relief at Tina and Chris. Tina knelt beside her friend and put her arms around her. In a few moments she was surrounded by her friends.

"Did he hurt you?" Pete asked her roughly, kneeling in front of her. She blinked at him, trying to stop shaking long enough to answer him, vaguely noticing that his face was smudged and scratched and his clothes were all dirty.

"N-no . . ." Was that her voice—that shaky, wobbly sound that was barely more than a whisper? Hot tears filled her eyes and began to race down her cheeks.

Pete's lips tightened, and she could see he was really angry.

"I'm-I'm sorry," she choked out. "I dropped my flashlight. . . . I couldn't see. . . . I called and nobody came. . . . It was too dark—" She stopped abruptly, aware she was babbling. Then she reached out and touched Pete's forehead. "You-you're bleeding . . . ?"

"The guy got in a lucky punch," he said, trying to smile but not quite succeeding. "But since he hit my head there isn't anything to worry about."

"Oh!" Jill's hand flew back to cover her face. "Oh, it's all my fault. . . . I'm sorry. . . . please, don't get mad at me. . . ."

Pete frowned—he'd never seen Jill so shook-up. He knelt there, watching her, chewing his lip, wondering what to do. Then he reached out to pat her awkwardly on the shoulder. "Aw, Jill, I'm not mad at you! I'm mad at that guy who grabbed you!" Before he knew what was happening, she turned and leaned against him, giving in to the sobs that were choking her. Looking at the others, his eyes filled with concern, Pete put his arms around her and tried to calm her down.

Willy watched, his teeth clenched so tight in anger

56

that his jaws ached. He put a hand on Chris's shoulder and felt that his friend was equally tense and angry.

"This is one adventure that got way out of hand," Chris said in a grim voice.

Willy nodded, jamming his hands into his pockets. He couldn't remember ever being as scared as he'd been when they'd come running up and realized Jill was really in trouble. "I couldn't believe it when I saw—" He broke off, and Chris looked at him.

"Yeah, me, neither."

"I think we should take Jill home," Tina said.

"I think we should call the police first," Jim said, looking down at Jill, who was starting to calm down.

Pete looked up at his friends, his eyes filling with anger.

"I think we should find that guy and teach him a lesson!" he said in a low, fierce voice.

The others looked at him, then at each other, shifting uncomfortably. Calling the police made the most sense . . . but they had to admit it would feel good to catch the creep who had scared Jill so badly. And maybe scare him just a little in the process, too.

CHOICE ⇒

If the gang decides to call the police, turn to page 92.
If they try to track down the guy first, turn to page 120.

Later, neither Chris nor Jim could remember who pushed who first. Could be that they pushed each other at about the same time. It didn't really matter. All they *did* know for sure was that things got out of hand. Way out of hand.

They pushed and punched each other until they both were bruised and bleeding. They might even have kept going if Jill hadn't come along.

"Are you two nuts?!" she yelled at them, unable to believe her eyes. They completely ignored her, until she calmly removed the lid from her super-biggie diet Coke with extra ice and lemon and doused them with it.

They jumped away from each other and stood there, staring at her, panting. She just looked them over and shook her head in disgust.

"Yeah, boy, you guys are just a great witness to anyone walking down the street." Her words all but dripped with sarcasm. "I mean, if you had to punch each other out, couldn't you at least pick a better place than right in front of the church?"

Chris swallowed painfully and sneaked a glance at Jim, who was sneaking a glance at him. Their eyes met, and both of their faces went bright red. Chris shook his head and stuck his hands in his pockets. "Oh man, Jim . . . I'm sorry . . . ," he said in a low voice.

Jim wiped Coke off his face, wishing he could wipe away his embarrassment as easily. "No, man, it's my fault. I shouldn't have pushed you."

"OK, so you're both jerks," Jill said, a smile tugging at her mouth. "How about shaking hands like good little boys and then we'll head to Chris's apartment so you can clean up. If your grandparents see you like this, Jim, you won't have to worry about getting clean. They'll just finish you off." Jim looked at her gratefully and reached out to shake hands with Chris.

"Good," she said, linking her arms in theirs and starting them toward Chris's apartment. "Now, you can tell me how you two got yourselves into this mess."

By the time they reached Chris's apartment, they had filled her in on everything. They were talking and laughing about the whole thing, but beneath their laughter, both Jim and Chris were still ashamed of what had happened. And they were uncomfortably aware that it was going to be awhile before they could forget what they had done and said to each other.

THE END

Turn to page 142.

Look, Rich, I know you're just trying to help us have fun," Chris said. "But I agree with Jim. This isn't something I want to do."

"Me, neither," Tina and Sam spoke together, then grinned at each other.

"We prefer scaring each other the old-fashioned way," Sam quipped.

Jill looked at Rich and smiled. "Sorry, but I guess we'll just go back to amusing ourselves with dumb stories."

He looked at them disgustedly, then stood. "Fine, you kiddies go back to your little bedtime stories. I thought you liked adventure and fun, but if you want to be a bunch of killjoys, so be it. Don't say I didn't try to enlighten you."

He turned and stomped back down the stairs.

The Ringers looked at each other. "Well, excu-u-u-se me!" Sam quipped. Everyone laughed and went back to their stories.

But somehow it didn't seem as much fun. Sam was just getting ready to launch into what he'd thought was a great story, but after a few words he just shook his head.

"I'm sorry, guys, but this just isn't fun anymore."

Chris nodded. "I know; I agree. All of a sudden it's like we're doing something that's not too cool."

"I think Rich did us a favor by coming up here," Tina said.

"How so?"

"Well, he made us take a look at what's fun and what isn't, and at what kind of fun is OK and what isn't. I don't see how telling stories about ghosts and monsters and the undead is that much different than what he was suggesting."

Willy nodded. "You're right. I guess we just wanted to do this so much that we ignored whether or not it was right. So, what do you say, Chris? This was your idea, and I don't want you to think we're just dumping on you."

Chris shrugged. "I say you guys are right. I guess there are just some things you have to stay away from if you want to please God."

"Well put, Reverend Martin," Jill teased, and Chris threw his pillow at her—which opened the door to a whole new activity! Suddenly the room was alive with flying pillows and hoots of laughter.

Now here's a game we can enjoy without feeling guilty! Jim thought with a smile. Then a huge pillow nailed him right in the face, and he jumped forward, intent on retaliation.

THE END

Have you visited the cemetery yet? Or encountered the Midnight Marauder? If not, go back to the beginning and see what those adventures are all about!

Chris stood up angrily. "Fine," he said. "If you guys are too scared to give this a try, then I'll do it on my own." He stomped out of the room and down the stairs, slamming the door to the church as he left.

"Well, that ended well," Sam said sarcastically.

"We can't just let him go," Jill said.

Jim got to his feet. "I'll go after him. This whole stupid idea was my fault anyway."

He went down the stairs and raced out the door—and tripped over Chris, who was sitting on the stairs, fuming.

"Whoa!" Jim yelled as he went airborne and tumbled onto the sidewalk below.

Through a haze Jim heard Chris's voice. "Jim! Are you OK?" He groaned and rolled over, staring up at the three Chrises who revolved above him.

"Hey, cool, how'd you do that?"

"Do what?"

"Never mind. But I always knew you were a schizophrenic. . . ."

After a few minutes, the world stopped spinning and there was only one Chris, so Jim reached out a hand. Chris helped him up, shaking his head, laughing. "Man, you should have seen your face!" he chuckled. "I've never seen your eyes open quite that wide."

"Yeah, well, you try flying without a net—or wings, or a plane, for that matter—and see what your eyes do."

They sat down on the stairs, neither one saying anything for a while. Finally Chris shrugged. "So, you think I've been stupid long enough and we can go back inside?"

"Sure, why not? We're always ready for a chance to forgive some poor slob who's done something really lame—"

He was cut off by Chris swatting at his arm, and he jumped up laughing. "I'm glad you decided against going after the marauder yourself, buddy."

Chris grinned sheepishly. "I had every intention of doing so, until I saw how dark it was, and how far away the cemetery was from everything, and how easy it would be for one Chris Martin to vanish without a trace in his quest for the marauder. So I figured, hey, let the police take care of him."

"That's what I like about you, Chris ol' boy!" Jim said, slapping him on the back as they walked up the stairs. "You've got an adventurer's spirit that just won't quit!"

Chris's only answer was a distinctly rude snort.

THE END

Turn to page 142.

With a sigh, Chris got up and left his room. He went down the hall quietly, listening. When he heard the water running in the kitchen, he knew the time had come. So he squared his shoulders and entered the room.

His mom was standing there, her hands buried in sudsy water. She glanced up when he came in, and an uncertain look crossed her face when she saw him. He tried to swallow, but suddenly there was a lump the size of New Jersey in his throat, so all he accomplished was to make himself cough and choke.

Mrs. Martin grabbed a towel and dried her hands off, then quickly led Chris to a chair at the table and gave him a glass of water. He reached for it thankfully, taking a few big gulps until he could breathe again. Then he glanced at her, and she grinned.

"You gonna make it?" she asked, the grin still tugging at her mouth.

He felt his own mouth starting to smile. "Yeah, I think so." Just then the phone rang, and Chris answered it.

"Oh, hi, Jim. What's up?"

"What are you doing right now," Jim asked.

"Well, I'm talking to my mom about something, but can I call you back?"

"I'm goin' over to the church now. Why don't you meet me there in about ten minutes.

"OK," Chris said, hanging up the phone. Glancing at the table, he noticed the book he'd been reading. The title's bloodred letters and the illustration of a ghostly vampire face with glowing, evil eyes stared back at him. He sighed and looked back at his mom. They both started talking at once.

"Mom, I'm really sorry—"

"Chris, about the book—"

They laughed, and Chris felt the heaviness that had been sitting on his heart starting to lift.

"Mom, I'm sorry about getting so mad. It's just that everybody at school is really into these books and stuff. They're always talking about them and about the shows they watch on TV. I mean, it's like some kind of national pastime, you know? And I feel like a real jerk because I'm the only one who's never read one of these things."

She raised an eyebrow in question. "The only one, huh? Do Jim and Willy read those books or watch those shows?"

Chris frowned, thinking. "Nnnnooo . . . I don't think so. . . ."

"How about Jill or Pete or Sam or—"

"OK, OK," he said, putting his hands up in surrender. "None of the Ringers are into them. Jill says they give her the willies." He grinned at his mom. "Of course, Willy says that just means they make her smart."

She smiled and nodded. That was exactly the kind of thing Willy *would* say. Then her face grew more serious. "Chris, what is it about these things that you like?"

He shrugged. "It's not that I like them. But everybody

else seems to, so I figured they knew what they were talking about and I was just . . . well, weird. But they're not so bad," he hurried on, seeing the look on her face and her raised eyebrows. "I mean, they look kinda cool, in a spooky way. Besides, good always wins over bad—and that's a good message, isn't it?"

"Sure it is," Mrs. Martin agreed. "But that's not always the message of these books, or of the TV shows."

Chris looked at her in surprise. "It's not?"

"Not by a long shot," she said.

To see what Mrs. Martin means, turn to page 29.

Chris and Tina walked slowly, shining their flashlights in a sweeping motion in front of them. It seemed as though they'd been looking forever, but it couldn't have been more than a few minutes. Chris glanced at Tina, wondering if she was still upset about the gang coming to the cemetery.

Well, there was only one way to find out.

"Tina?"

"Hmm?"

"Are you still mad . . . you know, about us coming here?"

She looked at him and stopped. "No, not mad. But . . . ," her voice trailed off.

"But?"

"But I think it's wrong." She spoke quietly, but firmly. "I mean, we're supposed to be doing things the way Jesus would do them, right? Isn't that what being a Ringer is all about?"

"Well, yeah. . . ."

"So why are we doing something that makes us liars? And trespassers? And lawbreakers, since you guys said it's against the law to be in here after dark? I sure don't think Jesus would do these kinds of things . . . or be very proud of us for doing them, either."

Chris listened quietly, his face growing warm as a terrible realization hit him: She was right—100 percent.

And he was wrong—200 percent, if there was such a thing, which there probably wasn't. But that didn't change the facts: He'd blown it.

He stared at the ground for a second and nodded. "You're right, Tina. We shouldn't be here. I guess I just figured we *could* do this, so we should. But it's not our job, is it?"

"I don't think so, Chris."

With a sigh, he lifted his whistle to his lips and blew, loud and long. Then he and Tina sat down on the ground to wait. He knew it wouldn't be hard for the gang to find them; they probably hadn't gotten that far away.

The hard part would be explaining to them that he was wrong and that they should head back to the church. He was pretty sure he'd get some arguments from the guys at least.

But he was wrong.

The gang had gathered within minutes, everyone asking what had happened and looking around nervously, expecting the see the marauder lurking somewhere nearby. Chris calmed them down, then briefly explained what he and Tina had talked about.

"So it took me awhile," he finally said, forcing himself to look them square in the eyes. "But I finally get it. We don't belong here. In fact, we're wrong to be here." He shook his head. "God isn't going to help us find this guy when we had to lie to be here in the first place."

Willy nodded. "I think you're right, Chris."

"You do?" Surprise—and relief—washed over him.

"Yeah, and so do I," Jill added. "The farther I walked,

the more anxious I felt. Like we were here to do something wrong instead of something good."

"Right," Pete said. "We can't expect God to agree with what we're doing if it's against his laws. And it's a whole lot more important that we're honest with Pastor Whitehead than it is for us to find this marauder. Agreed?"

A chorus of agreement went up. "So, back to the sleepover?" Chris questioned, feeling better already. Another chorus was raised, and they all moved together back to the church.

"Chris?" He turned to find Jim walking beside him.

"Yeah?"

"I'm going to tell Gramps what happened tonight. I think if we're going to be honest with him, we need to be honest all the way."

Chris was silent for a few heartbeats, then he nodded. "I'll go with you," he said firmly. "We thought this up together, so we'll confess it together." He grinned at Jim. "It feels so much better to admit we weren't alone when we did something really stupid!"

Jim laughed and ran up the steps of the church to let the others in. As Chris watched the Ringers go inside, he looked up at the moonlit sky. "Thanks, God," he whispered. "I guess you did answer my prayers after all."

THE END

Turn to page 142.

OK, Tina, everyone else has their assignments. Do you want to go or not?" Chris's voice broke into Tina's confused thoughts. She looked up, startled, and saw everyone staring back at her.

Taking a deep breath, she shook her head. "Not."

Chris blinked. "Not? As in you're not going?"

"Right. As in I'm not telling Gramps one thing and then doing another," she stated firmly, then looked at Jim, willing him to understand. "Grampa trusts us, Jim. But if we do this and he finds out, he sure won't trust us in the future."

"Well, who says he has to find out?" Sam offered, then felt his face redden when the others looked at him.

"Uh, yeah, no one has to tell him," Chris agreed lamely.

Jill shook her head.

"Yeah, and when we catch this marauder guy, how are we supposed to turn him over to the police without anyone knowing what we did?"

"Besides, I'm not so sure I like the idea of lying to Pastor Whitehead," Pete said quietly.

"Who said anything about lying?" Chris demanded, but Pete didn't back down.

"We told him we'd stay here, remember? If we don't, then we lied."

Chris wanted to argue, to say something that would make the adventure OK . . . but he couldn't. He leaned back against the wall with a frustrated sigh.

CHOICE

If Chris gives in, turn to page 95.

If he decides to go to the cemetery on his own, turn to page 61.

Finally Chris shrugged. "I suggested the stories, but it's not like we have to tell them or anything."

Jill nodded. "Right. I mean, if you'd rather not, there are a lot of other things we can do that would probably be more fun. I mean, I was never all that thrilled with the idea of the stories."

"You weren't?" Jim and Chris asked together in surprise.

She shook her head a little sheepishly. "I hate ghost stories and stuff like that," she said. "Nighttime is scary enough without thinking of witches and demons and gross stuff like that!"

"I'll go along with that," Sam agreed. "So what *do* we want to do?"

Pretty soon everyone was talking and coming up with new ideas. Tina just sat back and listened, a big grin on her face.

Later that night, just as she was slipping beneath the covers of her bed, there was a knock at her door. "Come in," she called.

Jim poked his head in the door, then came to perch on the edge of her bed. She pulled her knees up and hugged them.

"That was a pretty brave thing you did today," he said. She looked at him in surprise.

"What was?"

"Having everyone come over to talk about the overnighter. You were right, you know. Telling ghost stories wasn't a very good idea."

She grinned at him. "Yeah, I'm just glad everyone else agreed!"

He grinned. "Like they'd disagree with Princess Tina?"

"They just happened to recognize great wisdom when they heard it," she retorted.

"Nah, they just recognized there would be great hassles if they didn't agree with Her Highness."

"I'll give you 'Her Highness'!" She grabbed her pillow and clobbered him, knocking him off balance. With a whoop she jumped up and swung again, connecting this time with the side of his head and knocking him off the bed.

Warding off her blows, he lunged for her other pillow, and they launched into a full-scale battle. Finally they both lay on the floor, panting for breath and laughing.

"A wise princess *and* a fierce pillow warrior," Jim said laughing. "Oooh, I *am* impressed!" Tina just stuck her tongue out at him good-naturedly as he pulled himself to his feet and headed for the door. When he reached it, he paused and glanced back at Tina.

"I was just kidding about the hassles part, Tina."

She nodded. "I know."

"And I wanted you to know . . . well, I'm proud of you. You did a good thing."

His words really made her feel good and she smiled at him. "Thanks, big brother."

"Sleep well, Princess," he said with a grin, and left.

She gathered her pillows and crawled back under her covers, still smiling. "Thanks, God," she whispered. "You did a good thing."

THE END

Happy endings are always nice, but you don't have to stop here! There's still the Midnight Marauder, and the laser quest, and lots of other stories waiting to be read. Just turn back to the beginning and choose another choice!

Jill followed close behind Willy and Pete, her skin crawling with fear. She hadn't wanted to let any of the others know, but she hated the dark as much as Tina did. True, the moonlight was nice and bright, but still . . . there were weird shadows dancing all around them, especially on the gravestones.

"Nothing scary about a gravestone," she whispered to herself. "Just a place to put a name." To prove that to herself, she paused for a second and tried to read the name carved into the stone. "'Jill, Beloved Daughter, Taken from Us Too Soon'—" She broke off, disbelieving.

Her goose bumps grew into goose mountains, and she spun around to run after Pete and Willy. But in her haste, she ran into the unyielding concrete of the gravestone that was right behind her. With a thud she went down, sprawling on the ground—which wouldn't have been so bad except that her flashlight and whistle went sprawling, too.

She scrambled to her feet, looking around wildly. "Pete? W-Willy?" she called into the night—but the only sound that answered her was the sound of her own heart pounding.

She sank to the ground, surrounded by darkness, ignoring the cold seeping into her from the damp ground. She felt like she was going to scream.

CHOICE ⟹

If Jill screams, turn to page 20.

If she calms down and tries to figure out what to do, turn to page 43.

Cautiously, Chris moved forward, doing his best to be quiet, when—

Beep! Beep! Beep! his headgear came alive. Spinning around, he saw Willy standing there, aiming his laser gun at him.

"Oooh, you're dead, man!" Willy crowed in triumph.

"Stop goofing off," Chris scolded. "You're not even it."

Chris turned quickly to look for the figure, but there was no one there. Without even explaining to Willy what had happened, Chris pulled his headgear off.

He had to tell Pastor Whitehead.

He'd seen the Midnight Marauder!

Turn to page 52.

Before Chris could say anything, Pastor Whitehead put his fingers to his lips and motioned for Chris to follow him. They left as quietly as possible.

By the time they reached the cemetery entrance, the police were there. Pastor Whitehead went to speak with them, and Chris joined the other Ringers, who were bursting with excitement and curiosity.

"He was still there!" Chris crowed triumphantly, keeping his voice low.

"You're kidding!"

"What did he look like?"

"Did he see you?"

The questions came fast and furious, and Chris smiled smugly. "No, I'm not kidding. No, he didn't see us, and I'd say he was probably some kind of criminal on the run. You know, he had that desperate kind of look—"

"You're right about that, Chris, he did have a desperate look," said Pastor Whitehead. The Ringers gathered around him. "But not because he's a criminal."

"What do you mean, Grandpa?" Tina asked.

"Unless I miss my guess, the man we saw wasn't sneaking around in the cemetery. He was living there."

"*Living* there?" Pete echoed with disbelief. "Who would want to live in a cemetery?"

"Someone who doesn't have a home anyplace else,"

the pastor answered quietly. Stunned, the Ringers looked at him, then at each other.

"He's a homeless guy?" Chris asked.

"Yeah, that makes sense," Jim put in. "I mean, cemeteries don't exactly have a lot of people coming in and out after dark, so there wouldn't be anyone telling you to go away, you're not really in anybody's way, and it's nice and quiet."

"*Dead* quiet," Sam punned, and everyone groaned.

Chris glanced around and saw that the officers were gone, though their car was still in place. "Did the police go after the guy?"

"Yes," Pastor Whitehead said, nodding, "but not to arrest him. I gave them the phone number and address of a nearby shelter, and they're going to try to talk the man into calling me tomorrow. Depending on his circumstances, our church may be able to help him out with finding a job or a home, if he wants."

"That's a pretty big *if,* isn't it?" Jill asked. "I mean, if the guy wanted a job, wouldn't he already have one?"

"Not necessarily," Sam responded. "I know lots of people who want jobs and just can't find them."

"Not even at a McDonald's or something?"

He shook his head. "Not anywhere. Especially if you don't have a home. Lots of places aren't too thrilled about hiring someone who's homeless."

"But if they don't have jobs, how can they afford homes?" Willy asked.

"Bingo," Pastor Whitehead said. "It's a pretty vicious cycle. If you don't have a job, you can lose your home and end up on the streets. But if you live on the streets, employers don't trust you enough to give you a job, so you can't get the money to get off the streets." He looked at Jill. "See why it's not so simple after all?"

She nodded. "So, what can we do to help?"

"We've done all we can for this man tonight," Pastor Whitehead said. "But if you want, we can get together and talk tomorrow. There are shelters where the Ringers could volunteer to help. If nothing else, places like that are always in need of canned food, personal hygiene supplies—"

"What supplies?" Tina said, scrunching up her face.

"You know," Pete explained, "toothpaste, shampoo, deodorant—stuff like that."

"*Sparkly* toothpaste," put in Sam.

"Exactly." Pastor Whitehead smiled. "So, what do you say? Are you ready to find out what you can do to help?"

"Why not?" Tina said. "I mean, if we can catch the Midnight Marauder, we can do anything!"

"Right!" Willy agreed, then grinned and held his laser gun up. "But can we finish the game first?"

A chorus of agreement filled the air, and Pastor Whitehead laughed.

"Sure, I don't see why not!" He watched, smiling, as the gang scrambled to find the perfect hiding place.

Chris trotted into the woods, then ducked behind a large bush. As he crouched in the darkness, waiting for the signal to start the game, he started thinking. He was pretty lucky to have a loving mom and a safe, warm house, and all the stuff that made up his home. He made a vow to himself

80

that he would personally think of at least five ways the Ringers could reach out to help the homeless.

He grinned. Now *there* was an adventure waiting to happen—and one they could be proud of!

THE END

Turn to page 142.

Jim dropped to his knees in front of Chris and touched his forehead to the ground at Chris's feet.

"Yes, O Wise and Brilliant One! I acknowledge your greatness of mind, which is exceeded only by your greatness of humility."

"Har-dee-har-har," Chris said, nudging Jim with a foot. "So does this mean you like my idea or not?"

Jim looked up at him, his eyes sparkling with excitement. "When do we start?"

"All right!" Chris said, pulling his friend up. "The first thing we do is call the rest of the gang and then set up a plan."

"Don't you think we should talk with my grandfather and see if we can even do this? I mean, maybe he won't let us use the bell tower."

Chris pondered this, then shrugged. "I don't know. . . . I'd hate to have him tell us no when there's really no problem. I mean, we've been up here plenty of times to check the bells out. And it's not like you can fall out or anything. All the windows have glass in them."

"If we don't talk to Grandpa, how will we get in?"

"You have a key, don't you?"

"Well, yeah—"

"So, we use that to get in, and then to lock up in the morning. And no one ever even has to know we've been

here. It can be a . . . a secret meeting of the Ringers!" Chris
finished triumphantly.

Jim frowned. "I don't know, Chris. It sounds wrong
somehow."

CHOICE ⇔

If Jim and Chris decide to talk to Pastor Whitehead, turn
to page 110.

If they decide to make this a secret gathering, turn to
page 87.

Chris was silent for a few minutes, then he nodded. Might as well get it over with. His mom turned and led the way to the living room, where they sat down on the couch. He noticed the book he'd been reading was still there, staring up at him with the title's bloodred letters and the eerie, ghostly, vampire face with glowing, evil eyes.

"Chris," his mom started quietly, "I know you're not happy with my decision about the books—"

"Yeah, Mom," he broke in, "it just doesn't seem fair. I mean, everyone in the school reads those books or watches those movies on TV, and I feel like a total jerk when they ask me if I've read or seen them, and I have to say no."

Mrs. Martin thought for a minute, then asked, "Why do you think I object to those things?"

"'Cause you think they're gross," he said right away. "But you also get grossed out by the sludge in the bottom of the pitcher of orange juice, and just because you don't like something doesn't mean I won't."

"You're partially right. I do think the movies are gross." She smiled slightly. "Even more so than orange-juice sludge. And you're right that I shouldn't put something down just because I don't like it."

Chris looked at her in surprise. "You shouldn't?"

84

"Of course not. But Chris, there's more to these books and movies than just gross scenes."

"Like what?"

"Like the messages."

"But I don't read stuff or watch movies to get messages. They're just for having fun. And these things all look cool, in a spooky kinda way. Besides, good always wins over bad, and that's a good message."

"Yes, it is, but it's not always the message in these things."

Chris frowned. "It's not?"

"Not by a long shot."

 **CHOICE**

To see what Chris's mom means, turn to page 29.

Chris waited patiently for Jim to answer him. At least, Chris thought he was being patient. He didn't badger the guy or pin him up against the wall and demand an answer. But Jim's silence was really starting to get on his nerves—not to mention the self-satisfied smirk the guy had plastered on his face.

"Jim," Chris said, trying to keep irritation out of his voice. "Are you going to tell me about this marauder or not?"

"Maybe, maybe not," Jim said. This was really great! He had Chris right where—

"Fine, have it your way!" Chris's explosion cut off Jim's thought. And before Jim could stop him, Chris had stomped to the door, jerked it open, and stomped down the stairs.

"Hey—!" Jim stammered, then he ran after his friend. "Chris! Aw, come on! Wait a minute!"

But Chris didn't even slow down. He just kept walking, his shoulders stiff, his hands jammed in his pockets.

"Chris, come on! You know I was just giving you a hard time." Jim was walking beside him now, but Chris didn't even look at him. Jim reached out to grab Chris's arm to try and slow him down.

Chris jerked his arm away, which threw Jim off

86

balance so that he tripped and went sprawling on the
sidewalk. Chris managed to avoid stepping on Jim's head,
but just barely. For a second, Jim just lay there, stunned.
Then he was on his feet, standing toe to toe with Chris, a
furious look on his face.

They stood there, staring at each other angrily.

If the argument goes further, turn to page 57.

If the guys decide to calm down, turn to page 35.

Chris punched Jim in the shoulder. "Come on, you know we won't hurt anything. What can it hurt to have a secret meeting here?"

Jim looked at his friend and tried to come up with a good response, something that would make Chris see what a bad idea this was. But the only thing that came to his mind was *I don't like it.*

With a resigned shrug Jim muttered, "OK, OK. We'll do it your way." Then he fixed Chris with a glare. "But if Gramps finds out and we get in trouble . . . ," he began ominously.

Chris grabbed Jim's arm. "Don't worry about it! Let's go get the others!"

It didn't take long for word to spread about the secret meeting—two of the Ringers were gone, so it only had to spread to Willy, Jill, and Tina. Chris talked about it with such excitement and enthusiasm that everyone thought it was a pretty cool idea. Jim wished just one more person would agree with him—but no one said a word about whether or not it was right to sneak into the church.

They did decide, though, that having an overnight would be too tricky. Instead, they would tell their parents they were having a late show night. That way, they wouldn't be expected home until after midnight.

The night of the meeting, Jim and Tina headed out the door to meet the others at the church.

"Have a good time tonight," their grandfather called to them as they left. Jim glanced back, a guilty look on his face.

"Uh, yeah, thanks," he muttered, and hurried on.

"Oh, that was convincing!" Tina teased him. He didn't answer her. He was too busy feeling guilty again.

At the church, Jim unlocked the doors and they all slipped inside.

"No lights," Chris whispered, turning on a flashlight he'd brought. "We don't want anyone to see them from outside."

"What are you whispering for?" Willy asked. "There's no one here but us Ringers!"

They laughed and headed for the stairs to the bell tower. Soon they all were gathered at the top of the tower, looking out the windows.

"You can see for miles up here," Jill said, shining her flashlight out the window to see how far the light carried. Willy shone his light out, too, and suddenly they all joined in a My-Light-Shines-the-Farthest contest, except for Chris.

"Come on, you guys, knock it off," Chris finally said. "We don't want anyone to know we're here. Now let's get down to business."

They all gathered in a circle around the bell, which hung in the middle of the tower, but which was high enough that they could all see each other under it. "Everybody's lights off except mine," Chris said, and when all the lights were doused Chris grinned at his

coconspirators, the dim light of his flashlight reflecting on
his face.

"Now this is what I call a great idea!" he said, grinning.

Suddenly, a bright light cut through the darkness and
landed on Chris's startled face.

"OK, kids, just stay where you are!"

Every eye in the room flew to the doorway and
widened at the sight of the policeman standing there, a
stern look on his face, pinning them in the widespread
beam of his heavy-duty flashlight. He reached out to flick
on the light switch, then glanced at his partner, who stood
just behind him on the stairs.

"Better tell Pastor Whitehead we've found our
prowlers," he said, and the man nodded then headed down
the stairs. No one spoke, and within a few minutes, Pastor
Whitehead came through the doorway.

At the sight of the policemen, Jim had started to feel
sick. But when his grandfather entered the room and he
saw the look of surprise—and disappointment—on his
face, Jim just wanted to sink into the floor.

"I take it you know these kids?" the officer said to
Pastor Whitehead.

"I've always thought I did," he answered, his voice
hard. "Now . . ." He looked from one to the other, until his
gaze came to rest on Jim. "Now I'm not so sure."

The policeman nodded and slipped his flashlight into
a clip on his belt. "Well, I'll leave them to you, then, Pastor,"
he said, and the two officers moved down the stairs.

The silence in the room grew heavier with each

passing second. Finally Jim spoke up. "Grandpa, I'm sorry—" but Pastor Whitehead cut him off with a look.

"Pastor Whitehead, it's not Jim's fault," Chris said miserably.

"To be honest, Chris, I don't care whose fault this is. You all should have known better!" he responded sternly. "Mrs. Atkins across the street was scared silly when she saw the lights in the bell tower. She was sure the church was being robbed or vandalized."

"We were just having a meeting—," Chris started to explain, but another of those looks cut him off.

Pastor Whitehead stared at all of them for a few seconds, then shook his head. "I can't tell you how disappointed I am in you kids," he said, and they all stared at the floor, embarrassed and ashamed. "You've upset an elderly woman and caused the police to come out here when it wasn't necessary." He met Jim's eyes as he went on, "And you've all lied to your parents. That's not something any of us will forget for a long time. You've shown us we can't trust you to be where you say you are," he finished quietly. "And I can't help but believe your parents will be as hurt by that as I am."

Willy tried to speak up, to apologize, but his words caught in his throat at the look of disappointment in Pastor Whitehead's eyes. Tina sniffed and fought back tears, and she reached out for Jim's hand. He took it and looked at her, but there was nothing he could say.

"Come on, let's go to the office and call your parents," Pastor Whitehead instructed. The Ringers complied, still in silence. And as Jim moved down the stairs, he couldn't stop the tears from pooling in his eyes as he wondered how long it would take for his grandfather to trust him again.

THE END

A hard lesson for the gang, but it didn't have to end this way! Turn to page 110, or back to the beginning, to find a happier ending!

Chris looked at his friends, taking in the anger and fear on the faces around him. This whole crazy game had been his idea. Now . . . now he needed to do something smart, for a change.

"Willy, you come with me," he said, meeting Pete's eyes evenly. "There's a pay phone in the parking lot. We'll call the police."

Anger flashed in Pete's eyes, then he looked away and breathed deeply. Chris waited. He wasn't going to tell Pete not to be mad. Shoot, he was so mad himself he could punch a hole through something. But he wasn't sure who he was really mad at . . . the guy who'd grabbed Jill, or himself.

After a few seconds, Pete looked back at him and nodded curtly. "Go ahead. Jim and I will stay with the girls until the police come."

It didn't take long for the police to get there. They talked to each of the kids, asking them what had happened, why they'd been in the cemetery, what Jill's attacker had looked like. Then they put Jill, her pale face smudged with dirt and tears, in one of the squad cars and took her home. The gang stood watching, silent, as the car pulled away. Finally, a tall officer came to talk to them, his voice and eyes stern.

"You know, you kids are lucky. This could have ended a lot differently."

Chris stuck his hands in his pockets, fighting the lump that had been rising in his throat for the last hour.

"I'm half tempted to write you all citations for breaking curfew and trespassing—" seven pairs of eyes flew to his face, widened in alarm—"but I think you've learned your lesson already." He smiled briefly at the relief that washed over the young faces in front of him. "OK, we've had the station call your parents, and they'll be here soon to get you." He turned away brusquely, before any of the group could see his smile broadening at the expressions on their faces when they heard their parents had been called.

"Oh, man," Willy groaned. "I may as well forget about college, 'cause I'll be an old man with a beard down to my toes before my folks ever let me out of the house again."

"Yeah, and we'll be lucky ever to see each other again," Sam said glumly. "I can just hear the old 'if-your-friends-jumped-off-a-cliff-would-you-jump-too?' lecture revving up."

Chris nodded miserably, unable to think of a clever comeback for his friends. He was too busy thinking of how he was going to have to tell his mom this whole evening had stemmed out of one of his "genius" ideas.

Jim and Tina looked at each other and sighed. They knew they wouldn't fare any better than Chris or Willy. Let's see, trespassing, out after curfew, breaking a promise to stay at the church . . . oh yes, they were in for a long night.

94

Pete watched his friends silently. He didn't know what his parents would say, but he did know this: It wouldn't be any worse than what he had been saying to himself for the last few hours. And it could never be worse than what he had felt when he came around the corner and saw that guy shaking Jill until he had thought her head would snap off. He closed his eyes, wishing that image would just go away.

But he knew it wouldn't. Not for a very, very long time.

THE END

Turn to page 142.

Chris listened to the discussion in the room for about ten minutes. Finally, he couldn't take it anymore. "OK, you win," he said in a grumpy voice. "We'll stay here. But you guys have really blown this one. We could have had a great adventure."

Jill patted him on the arm. "Maybe so," she said. "But I'd hate to be the one to try and explain our adventure to Pastor Whitehead."

"What adventure is that?"

Everyone turned, startled. There, standing in the doorway, was Pastor Whitehead, smiling at them.

Chris's face was a study in embarrassment. "Uh, well, nothing . . . ," he stammered.

Tina felt sorry for him—after all, he *had* agreed to forget about his adventure—so she jumped up and went to hug her grandfather. "What are you doing here?" she asked, smoothly changing the subject.

He grinned at her. "I've brought you a surprise!" And with that, he held out several large bags. The Ringers scrambled over to him, taking the bags and pulling out the contents.

"Lazer Tag!" Chris exclaimed. "You brought us the stuff to play Lazer Tag!"

"One of the church members heard about your overnighter here," he said, laughing at their excitement, "and he thought you'd all have fun with these. We'll keep the equipment here at the church to use for youth gatherings." He held up one of the green guns and its headset. "But for now, let's give these things a test run!"

They all whooped and cheered, then followed Pastor Whitehead down the stairs and outside. There was a park in front of the church that had some trees, some large rocks, and a clearing in the center. Folks called it the Common. Behind the church, on the other side of an alley, was the cemetery.

Chris gazed in the direction of the cemetery, tempted to *wander* in that direction.

"Come on, Sherlock," Willy said, grabbing Chris's arm, "forget about the marauder. We've got some lasering to do!" With a reluctant glance back at the cemetery, Chris followed his excited friend.

Within moments, each Ringer was decked out in a headset—which was composed of two plastic straps, one to circle the head front to back and the other to go over the top of the head, and a target unit on the side that had a 360-degree infrared sensor. A thin wire connected the headset to the fluorescent-green laser gun, which was complete with hand grips, a switch to change the infrared beam from wide to narrow, a single-shot or rapid-fire selector switch, and an amplification speaker that let everyone hear, loud and clear, the sounds of the battle.

Willy and Chris jumped around, acting like Super Ninjas and shooting at each other. Willy's target unit on his headset lit up, showing a hit.

"Whoa! This thing vibrates!" Willy yelped, laughing.

"Right," Pastor Whitehead said. "It's so you can feel it when you're hit. Your guns also vibrate and light up when they're hit, and even show how much damage was done."

"This is too cool!" Pete said. The others grinned at him, knowing how much he loved anything and everything electronic.

"So, who's going to be it first?" Chris asked.

"I'll be it," Sam said, stepping forward. "But not for long," he added, waving his gun in a threatening manner, and the others laughed.

"OK, here's how these things work," Pastor Whitehead explained. "When you fire, aim for the headsets or the guns. Like Willy said, you'll hear and feel it when you've been hit. And when you're hit, you're it. You've each got six shots before your guns shut off automatically. When your shots run out, you're out of the game."

"Six shots doesn't seem like much!" Jill said, and Pastor Whitehead nodded.

"It wouldn't be if the gun was out for good, but all you have to do is turn it on again, and you've got another six rounds." He looked at Willy and Chris. "Since you two have already used up several shots, why don't you go ahead and use the rest so we can see what happens."

They gladly demonstrated, shooting at everyone until their guns suddenly shut down. They flipped their guns back on and jumped when the guns erupted in loud electronic whoops and whistles.

"Guess you can't cheat in this game, huh?" Sam said, grinning. "You'd know from a mile away that someone had to turn his gun back on!"

"Exactly," Pastor Whitehead agreed. "So use your six shots wisely. OK, spread out, and don't go beyond the field. I'll count to one hundred, then blow this whistle. When you hear that, the game is on!"

"How will we know the game is over?" Pete asked, always the one for getting as much detail as possible.

"Good question." Pastor Whitehead thought for a minute. "How's this? I'll do one long whistle for the start of the game and several short blasts to let you all know the game is over and you need to come back to the clearing."

"Works for me," Willy said, and the others nodded.

The Ringers scattered, each looking for the best hiding place for an ambush. Chris and Willy headed in the same direction, then broke off. Chris hesitated, then moved toward the edge of the field closest to the cemetery. He knew he should stay away from it, but he just couldn't help himself.

He passed the Freeze and reached the waist-high, wrought-iron fence that surrounded the cemetery and stood there, watching. After a few seconds, he shook his head.

"There's nothing there, Martin," he muttered to himself. "Go play tag." He started to turn, then froze.

Someone was there, standing by a gravestone, watching him.

Chris blinked his eyes, then looked again.

The form was still there, still watching.

OK, Sherlock, he thought, using Willy's nickname for him, *what do you do now?*

CHOICE ➤

If Chris tries to find out who is in the cemetery, turn to page 76.

If he goes to tell the others what he's seen, turn to page 52.

Tina looked down and closed her eyes, swallowing a scream and trembling. She *wanted* to look up, but for some reason she couldn't. She felt paralyzed. *Look up,* she told herself, but her body wouldn't move. Seconds went by. *Look up!*

Tina slowly opened her eyes. She looked at the floor and automatically grabbed for her flashlight. As soon as she had it in her hands, she shined it through the doorway and down the stairs.

There was nothing there!

A hand on her shoulder made her scream and spin around.

"Whoa, Sis!" Jim said, laughing. "What's wrong, did you think you'd been had?"

She pushed his hand away angrily and pointed at the doorway. "There was someone there!"

Jim's eyebrows shot up in disbelief as Chris came to join them.

"Who?" he asked.

"How should I know? It was dark!"

He looked at her doubtfully, and she stomped her foot in frustration. "I'm telling you, there was someone there, and he . . . or she . . . or *it* was watching us!"

"Maybe we'd better go find Rich," Jill suggested. Tina glanced at her gratefully.

Chris reached out and turned on the light. "No problem," he said. "He should be in the office."

Chris, Jim, and Tina were elected to go find Rich. Sam, Jill, and Willy were to stay in the bell tower and clean up the mess they'd made. Jill grimaced. "How is it that I always end up cleaning up after you guys?" she muttered as the others started down the stairs.

"Just lucky, I guess," Chris answered over his shoulder.

The three delegates reached the office and tapped on the closed door. No answer. Jim and Chris looked at each other, and Jim knocked harder. Still no answer.

Tina felt chills going up her spine again and reached out to slip her hand into Jim's. "Maybe he's asleep," she whispered uncertainly.

"Only one way to find out," Chris said and opened the door. He flipped on the light switch, then blinked at what he saw. The office was empty.

"Didn't Rich say he was going to stay right here?" Jim asked, frowning.

"Yeah," Chris agreed. "That's what he said." He looked around curiously. "There's no sign of his sleeping bag or his books. This is too weird! Let's go back upstairs."

He turned and ran back up the stairs—where he found a completely empty room! All the stuff was still there, but all the Ringers were gone! He turned on the lights to be sure they weren't just hiding.

Nope. He was the only one there.

The only one . . . ?

He ran back to the stairs. "Tina? Jim?"

No answer.

"Come on, you guys, this isn't funny!" Chris said, trying to keep his voice from shaking. He couldn't decide if he was angry or terrified. Either way, it didn't feel good. He turned on the stairway light—he didn't want darkness anywhere—and went back down to the office.

Empty.

"Oh man, oh man!" he muttered. "What's going on here?"

Suddenly, all the terrifying images from the stories he'd heard earlier started to swim through his mind. No matter what he told himself, he was sure there was someone, somewhere, just waiting to get him.

"I'm—I'm the last Ringer," he whispered into the darkness. He lifted the phone to call Pastor Whitehead, but all he heard was silence. The phone was dead. His mouth went dry and his hands started to shake. With a muffled groan, he ran upstairs again to search the other rooms. But when each one was as empty as the last, he started to wonder if some of those stories weren't really happening.

With a yell, he raced to the foyer and the familiarity of the doors leading to the sanctuary. "Watch my back, you guys!" he muttered to the carvings of a lion and a lamb in the wooden doors, then pulled them open and went in.

Immediately something grabbed him from behind, uttering an awful, guttural howl as it dragged him back into the foyer.

Chris had no choice. He did what any courageous, confident adventure-lover would do: He screamed. Loud. And when he hit the floor, he curled up into a ball, covering his head with his hands.

That's when he heard it. Laughter. All around him. Peeking through his eyelids, he looked up—and saw the Ringers and Rich all circled around him.

Furious, he jumped to his feet.

"Are you guys crazy?" he yelled. "You could have given me a heart attack!"

"No way, Chris," Tina said, grinning. "But what we *did* give you was exactly what you said you wanted tonight: a good scare."

"Yeah," Sam added. "You were so set on this monster story marathon, that we decided we'd go you one better. So, how did you like, Kimosabe?"

Chris stared at them. His breathing and heart rate were starting to return to normal. He knew he could get angry. Really angry . . . but he couldn't deny the fact that they were right. He *had* pushed for the stories, and for getting scared. Even when most of the others said they'd rather not do it. He shook his head and laughed ruefully.

"How did I like it? I hated it!" The gang laughed and high-fived each other. "I think it gave me enough 'scared' to last me three lifetimes."

"Good," Jill said with satisfaction. "Now maybe we can do something really fun."

"Such as?" Chris challenged. And she held out her flashlight.

"Such as flashlight tag in the Common! Rich called Pastor Whitehead, and he said it would be OK as long as we stay in the clearing."

A few minutes later, everyone was outside, having a

104

blast. And as Chris ran, trying to duck the beam of someone's flashlight, he made a deal with himself.

From now on, the scariest thing he would do, read, or watch, was "The Three Stooges Meet Frankenstein."

Somehow, that just seemed a lot more sensible.

THE END

Well, this adventure is over. But there are a lot more to go! Turn back to the beginning and make some new choices to see what happens when the group tries to track down the infamous Midnight Marauder.

Well, Tina, what's it going to be?" Chris asked.

"OK, let's do it your way," she said.

"All right, Tina!"

"I knew you wouldn't let us down!"

"Good girl, Tina!"

The others all gathered around her, slapping her on the shoulder and generally making her feel pretty good. But as she settled down to listen to Chris's plan, she couldn't keep a nagging voice from digging at her.

This isn't right! it kept saying.

"Oh, shut up!" she muttered fiercely, and Chris looked up from his maps in surprise. Tina blushed and shook her head. "No, no, not you, Chris."

He shrugged and went on. "OK, everyone gets a flashlight, a whistle, and a squirt gun. We'll split into two teams of two and one team of three, right? And each team will get a map. We'll cover our assigned areas, then report back at the gate in a half hour. If no one has seen anything, we'll switch maps and try again. Got it?"

"What do we do if we find this guy?" Jill asked.

"Squirt him if you can, then give a whistle. The rest of us will come running. Any other questions? No? Then let's go!"

Within minutes, each of the Ringers had grabbed the

appropriate gear and run down the stairs and out of the
church into the dark moonlit night.

The cemetery was dark and still when the Ringers arrived.
A full moon illuminated everything with an eerie glow,
casting slanting shadows that made the black wrought-iron
fence look tall and menacing. It was only waist high, but
somehow the darkness made it seem taller. As the Ringers
carefully pushed the gate open, it gave a mournful
squeak—making several of the adventurers jump a foot.
Once inside, they gathered near a large gravestone that
looked like a tall pillar topped with the figure of an angel.
The air was warm and humid, and there was a mist hanging
close to the ground.

All in all, it looked pretty freaky.

The gang gathered in a circle, and everyone looked
around nervously. Everyone, that is, except Chris. It didn't
even seem to bother him that he was in a cemetery in the
middle of the night.

Tina was especially nervous. She hated the dark. But
what she hated even more than the dark was being in the
dark surrounded by gravestones and weird looking statues!
She clenched her hands together to keep them from
shaking and looked over her shoulder.

"Auugh!" she screamed, for there, behind her, was a
hideous form reaching out to grab her!

"Auugh!!" Everyone else screamed in reaction. Some
of them dove for the nearest hiding place—which
generally tended to be a gravestone. Others just grabbed
each other and jumped a mile into the air.

"What?!" Jim said, looking at Tina like she was crazy. "What's wrong?"

Tina pointed at the figure behind her, and Jim shone his flashlight in that direction, the beam slicing through the darkness to reveal a large marble angel balancing atop a family memorial. Its arms reached out as though to embrace whoever was standing in front of it.

"An angel?!" Chris said, peering out from behind the gravestone he'd chosen as shelter. "You scared us all silly because you saw an angel?"

Tina felt the hot color rush into her face, and she rounded on Chris angrily. "Yeah, well, it didn't look like an angel when it was dark, OK? Besides, you ran for cover fast enough, so don't try to pull your Mr. Bravery stuff on me!"

Chris opened his mouth to make a cutting retort, but Willy put his hand on his arm.

"Come on, you guys. Let's not fight."

"Yeah," Jill said. "If you guys are going to fight, I'm going home." She looked around uncertainly. "Besides, I'm not so sure anymore that this was a very good idea."

"Of course it isn't a good idea," Chris replied. "It's a *great* idea. You girls just don't recognize genius when you encounter it." He turned to Willy and Sam. "OK, you guys, you have your assignments, right? So move out."

"Us? Why do we have to move out first?" Willy protested.

"Yeah," Sam agreed, peering into the darkness surrounding them. He just *knew* there was something out there waiting to get him, and he was in no hurry to give it its chance. "This is your great idea, Mr. Genius, so why don't *you* head out first and show us how it's done?"

"Come on, you guys! What are you, chicken?"

"No more so than you are, Mr. You-Go-First-I'm-Right-Behind-You."

Tina listened to them going back and forth, then shook her head. What were they doing out here, in the dark, surrounded by gravestones and dead people!? Shivers of fear ran up her spine and she hugged herself.

"Can we pray about this?" she asked in a small voice. Chris, Willy, and Sam stopped their arguing and looked at her.

"Pray?" Chris said.

"Yeah," Sam retorted, "you know, folding your hands, talking to God, asking him to keep you alive . . . pray."

"Good idea," Willy said, and the others agreed. They stood in a circle, holding hands.

"OK," Chris said, looking at his friends. "Who wants to pray?"

"You do," Sam said.

Chris started to protest, then clamped his mouth shut and nodded. They all bowed their heads.

After a few seconds, Chris started praying. "God, please help us find the marauder. . . ."

Do you really think God will help you do that? He paused, frowning. He'd heard his conscience often enough to recognize its interference right away. He considered the question carefully. They were just trying to help the police . . . but they had lied in the process. . . .

"Uh . . . well, help us to do the right thing. . . ."

If you did that, you wouldn't be here!

"Keep us safe. Amen." He finished quickly and dropped the hands he'd been holding. He glanced up and met Tina's eyes—then looked away.

The Ringers broke up into their teams—Willy, Pete, and Jill; Sam and Jim; Chris and Tina—and headed out.

CHOICE

If the Ringers have second thoughts about this adventure, turn to page 66.

If they go through with it, turn to page 74.

Chris watched Jim closely and saw the uncertainty on his face. He looked as if he wished he could just forget about the whole thing.

"OK, OK," Chris said in a resigned tone. "I guess you're right. So we talk with your grandfather first."

Jim looked at his friend and smiled gratefully. "Great. Let's go. I think he's home right now."

Pastor Whitehead listened carefully as Jim and Chris outlined their idea. They left out the part about the scariest story contest. They just told him they wanted to have an all-nighter in the bell tower. After they'd given him their best, most convincing pitch, they sat back and waited.

Leonard Whitehead, Jim's grandfather, was a good friend to all the Ringers. He had worked as a missionary in Brazil for many years. Then just a few years ago, he retired and came to Millersburg to reopen their church. The Ringers all thought of him as their pastor—but they had known about him long before he came to town because of his sister, Miss Whitehead. She had been Chris and Willy's favorite Sunday school teacher. She seemed to know the whole Bible by memory and loved to have contests with the kids in her classes to see who could find a verse in the Bible the fastest or who could be the first to correctly recite a verse. She'd made Sunday school so much fun that all of the kids looked forward to it. In fact, she was the one who'd given them the idea of being the Ringers in the first place. She'd told them that a "ringer" was someone who looked just like someone else. So she thought it would be great to be a "ringer" for Christ.

Miss Whitehead's death had been hard for Chris and Willy, but sometimes it was almost as if she were still around because they remembered her so well.

Later, after she died, Mr. Whitehead arrived, and he asked the gang to ring the church bell every Sunday. That's how they became known as the Ringers.

Now, as Chris waited for Pastor Whitehead's decision, he noted how much the man looked like Miss Whitehead. That was probably because they'd been twins—but Chris figured it was also because they both loved God so much.

"Well, boys," Pastor Whitehead said, watching their half-expectant, half-fearful faces. "I sure don't see any reason why you couldn't have an overnight in the tower."

"YES!" Chris yelped, jumping up and giving Jim an excited high five.

"I only have two conditions," Pastor Whitehead continued, smiling. Chris and Jim stopped at the word *conditions,* glancing at each other in a worried manner. "Don't worry," Pastor Whitehead said with a chuckle, "they're not too tough. First, you each have to get a signed OK from your parents."

"No sweat," Jim said.

"Second, I'd like an adult to be at the church while you're there." The boys started to protest, but Jim's grandfather just held up a hand. "You don't have to invite him—or her, as the case may be—to your party. But I want someone there who will know what to do if there's trouble of any kind. So what do you say? Sound fair?"

Chris and Jim looked at each other, then nodded. "It's a deal," Chris said.

"Good. Just bring the signed permission sheets to me, and the name of the person who will stay at the church with you. I'll want to meet him or her before the overnight, so you'd better get busy."

Jim and Chris walked to their bikes, talking excitedly about their plans. Suddenly Chris stopped.

"I've got it!" he said.

"Well, don't give it to me!" Jim retorted.

"No, no. I mean, I know who to get to stay at the church with us."

"Who?"

"Jill and I have a friend at school whose older brother is going to be a minister. He's even been at the seminary for a year already. So he ought to be a good candidate for a watchdog. What do you think?"

"Sounds good to me," Jim agreed.

Plans for the overnight proceeded quickly and smoothly. Rich Allen, the seminary student, agreed to stay at the church with the gang. He met with Pastor Whitehead, who approved him—though it seemed to Jim he did so without real enthusiasm. That was kind of strange, but he got caught up in the overnight plans and didn't think of it again.

At least, not until the night of the overnight.

Once the chaperon was found, Jim and Chris called the

others in the gang. No one seemed real excited about the idea of the stories, but Chris badgered them until everyone agreed to give it a try. Everyone, that is, but Tina. When Jim told her what Chris had in mind, she just looked at him.

"A scariest story contest? Why would we want to sit around at night and tell scary stories? I don't think that sounds like fun at all. Who wants to be scared, especially in that dark, old bell tower? Besides, I don't think it sounds like something the Ringers should be doing."

"What's that supposed to mean?" Jim questioned.

"I don't know," she said, her face growing red, an uncomfortable feeling stirring around inside her. "I just don't think Gramps would like it if he knew why we wanted to do this. You know how he feels about reading or watching things that are spooky or weird."

" 'Fix your thoughts on what is true and good and right,' " Jim quoted.

" 'Think about things that are pure and lovely, and dwell on the fine, good things in others,' " Tina joined in.

Grinning at each other, they finished together: " 'Think about all you can praise God for and be glad about it,' Philippians, chapter four, verse eight."

Jim nodded. "I know, but all we're doing is telling stories. That's not 'dwelling' on anything. It's just having fun."

Tina shook her head, and a scowl crossed Jim's face.

"Look, just because you're scared of your own shadow when the lights go out doesn't mean the rest of us can't have some fun. Lighten up, Tina."

"I am *not* scared!" she huffed. "And if the lights were out, there wouldn't be any shadows, Mr. Know-It-All."

With that parting shot, she turned her back on him and stomped into the living room. Dropping onto the couch, she turned on the TV. But she wasn't really paying attention to what was on. She was too busy thinking about what Jim had said.

If she was honest, she had to admit he was right. She *hated* the dark; it scared her. She could still remember all the strange sounds she'd heard at night in the jungle when she lived in Brazil. Sometimes it even sounded like people screaming. . . . Her parents had always told her the sounds were animals or birds. And they prayed with her, asking God to help her not be afraid. Still, when it got dark, it didn't take much to get her scared. And she hated being scared.

Then there was the part about not telling her grandpa what they were doing. She was *sure* he wouldn't like the idea. "I bet if I told him what was going on, he'd tell Jim we couldn't do it." But if she told Gramps about the contest, Jim and the others would just think she was a tattletale.

"Since when are you interested in professional wrestling?"

Her grandpa's question, which came from behind her, made her jump. She glanced from him to the TV. Sure enough, there were three big guys all decked out in their weird wrestling outfits, their faces all painted up so that they looked like they should be part of some heavy metal group, slamming each other into the floor of the wrestling ring. With a disgusted snort, Tina zapped the remote and sent Dr. Death and the Zombie Squad into TV oblivion.

Her grandfather chuckled and came to sit beside her on the couch.

"So, are you ready for the big overnighter at the church?" he asked. Tina's eyes widened. She couldn't have asked for a more perfect opening. All she had to do was open her mouth and tell him what was going on.

Instead, she just sat there, her mouth hanging slightly open, trying to think of what to say.

"Tina, are you OK?" her grandfather asked, looking at her curiously.

CHOICE ➡

What do you think? Should Tina tell her grandfather about the scariest story contest? If so, turn to page 22.

If not, turn to page 139.

Hurry up, Tina," Jim said from the bottom of the stairs. "We're supposed to be at the church in ten minutes!"

"OK, OK, I'm coming!" Tina grabbed her pillow, sleeping bag, and backpack and hurried down the stairs, almost tripping in the process. She followed Jim out the door and into their grandfather's waiting car.

Within minutes, they had joined the rest of the gang at the church. Tina's grandfather hugged her good-bye and grinned at her.

"You kids have fun tonight," he said. "But not *too* much fun! We'd like the church to be standing in the morning." He winked as he got back in his car and drove away. Tina stood watching him leave, trying to stifle the stab of guilt she felt. She wished she'd told her grandpa what they were planning to do. Maybe he would have laughed and said it sounded like fun, and then she wouldn't have to feel like she was doing something not quite right.

"Yeah," she muttered to herself as she pulled the door open and went into the building. "Or maybe he would have told us this was as bad an idea as I think it is. And then I wouldn't be in this mess." She turned and went to join the others, who were farther inside the church now.

Rich Allen was talking with Chris, asking him their

plans for the evening. Chris was doing a good job of answering while still being vague.

"Well, if you need me I'll be bunking in the office," Rich said, a slight grin on his face. "That way I'll be near the phone, and I can study to my heart's content." He patted a pile of thick books resting on a small table by the doors to the sanctuary.

"I'll let the others know," Chris said. "But I'm sure we'll be fine."

Yeah, right, Tina thought as she climbed the stairs to the bell tower. *Scared spitless, but fine.*

The others had already staked out their sleeping spots, and she moved to spread out her sleeping bag beside Jill's. All the Ringers except Pete were coming. He was out of town with his parents.

For the first hour or so everyone was too busy eating munchies and drinking pop to tell any kind of stories. Then Chris walked over to the light switch and turned it off. The room was plunged into total darkness.

"Hey! Turn that back on!" Jill screeched. "I don't have my flashlight out!"

Chris obliged, grinning at the others. "Just wanted to get your attention," he said smugly. Someone threw a pillow at him, which he dodged with ease. "Come on, guys, it's contest time," he said, and they all pulled out their flashlights and gathered in a circle. Once more Chris turned off the lights, but this time the room was dimly lit by flashlights. He plopped down beside Jim.

"Who's first?" Chris asked, looking around expectantly.

"I'll go," Sam said. His story was a little scary, but not

too bad. Then Willy went, and his story—about a psychotic killer who preyed on kids who were out after dark—sent chills up and down her spine. She found herself glancing at the shadowed doorway every few seconds, straining to hear if anyone was creeping up on them as they sat there.

"Chill, Tina!" Chris said, laughter in his voice. She looked at him, embarrassed. "You act like a little kid who's afraid of the dark." He looked at the others. "Who's next?"

"I've got one, provided Miss Herky-Jerky can calm down and stop jumping at every little sound," Jill said sarcastically. Tina looked down, fighting tears.

Jill launched into a terrible story about ghosts and hauntings and weird things happening to some poor helpless girl while she was baby-sitting. Just as Jill got to an especially scary part, Tina glanced at the doorway again—and her heart seemed to stop.

There, silhouetted in the doorway, was a tall, still form. Tina blinked her eyes once . . . twice . . . but the form was still there, watching them. She grabbed Jim's arm, and he yelped and jumped—which spooked the others so that they all yelped and jumped too, knocking over their flashlights and cans of pop and sending bowls of popcorn flying.

Tina scrambled after her rolling flashlight . . . then froze when she realized it had taken her right to the feet of the shadowy form! Slowly she looked up, not sure if she was going to scream or faint.

CHOICE ⟹

If Tina tries to regain her composure first, turn to page 100.

If she decides to scream, turn to page 11.

Chris stood silent for a minute, looking at the others. He glanced at Pete, and when their eyes locked, he nodded slightly.

"Jim, you and Tina take Jill home. The rest of us will follow in a few minutes."

Tina looked at Chris in surprise. "Chris, you're not going to—" Then, seeing the looks on the guys' faces, she broke off, biting her lip. They wouldn't listen to her.

"Come on, Tina," Jim said, touching her arm. "Let's get Jill home."

She glared at the guys for a second, then, muttering "You guys are making a mistake," she reached down to help Jill stand up.

As soon as Jill, Jim, and Tina were out of sight, Pete stood and faced the others.

"I saw where he headed when we showed up. Follow me." He started walking, and the others followed. It was only a few minutes before Pete stopped and motioned to Chris and Sam and Willy. Cautiously, they moved to stand beside Pete, and he pointed.

Chris peered into the dark distance, and spotted it: a small fire—a campfire, from the looks of it—right in front of one of the largest gravestones in the cemetery. Frowning, Chris looked at Willy. What kind of criminal camped out in a cemetery?

As they inched forward, Chris's heart started to pound so hard he was sure the guy they were sneaking up on would hear it.

What are we doing?! he wondered to himself, remembering how big the guy was. A hand clasped his arm, and he jumped in alarm.

"Shhh!" Willy hissed at him. "Sam wants us to circle around." Chris nodded, and he and Willy headed for the other side of the grave marker. They were close enough now to see the man sitting near the fire, his shoulders hunched. Chris crouched down and tried to get a good look at the guy. That was all they needed, a good look so they could get a description of the guy to give the police.

He was just starting to get a cramp in his leg from not moving when the guy looked up—and stared right at Chris and Willy.

"Stop hiding out there! You want me, then you come get me!" he boomed out in a deep voice.

Before the two startled friends could move, the man jumped to his feet and came after them. In their attempts to scramble out of the way, they tripped over each other—and then it was too late. He had grasped each one by the arm and dragged them back toward the fire.

"Let go!" Chris yelped as Willy kicked out at the man's legs desperately. Then two forms shot out of the darkness and hit the man square in the back, knocking all of them to the ground.

Pete and Sam!

Willy and Chris scrambled to their feet and jumped back into the mass of grunting, struggling forms. Within minutes, they had the man pinned down. Pete and Sam each held an arm, while Chris and Willy sat on his legs.

Chris looked at the attacker—a shock ran through Chris. It was an old man!

At least, he looked old. His face was wrinkled and dirty, and his matted hair stuck out from under a POW baseball hat that had somehow stayed on his head during the struggle. His eyes were all red, and he blinked at them like an owl. His clothes were torn and ragged—and looked as though they'd never seen a washing machine close up.

"Owww!" the man howled. "Why you hurtin' me? Why you chasin' me? This is my digs, you go find your own!"

"Your digs?" Pete asked, frowning.

"My digs, *my* digs," the man repeated in a singsong kind of voice, then whimpered. "This is my home. No one to mess with me. No one to bother me. 'Cept you kids. But I ain't leavin'. You go away. Leave me be. . . ."

He rattled on in a whiny voice, and the four Ringers looked at each other, shaking their heads.

"If we let you go, do you promise not to run?" Pete asked.

"Or come after us?" Willy added quickly.

The man stilled, looked at them, then nodded. Slowly the four boys backed away from the man, and he sat up.

"What are you doing here?" Pete asked.

"Livin'," the man answered simply.

"Why would anyone live in a cemetery?" Willy said.

"No place else to live," he said, and went to put another stick on his fire, completely ignoring the boys standing there gawking at him. It was as though they didn't even exist. Finally Chris walked up to him and asked softly, "Why did you grab Jill? You remember, the girl you grabbed a few minutes ago?"

He kept staring into the fire. "She scared me. I thought she was coming to tell me to leave." His red eyes suddenly seemed to fill with tears. "Wouldn't have hurt her. Just wanted her to go away." He turned and looked into Chris's eyes, and Chris was shocked at the pain he saw there. "Just want to be left alone," the man said in a low voice.

Chris felt a hand on his shoulder and looked up to find Pete standing there, motioning for him to follow him. He rose, and Pete leaned toward the man. His anger was gone.

In its place was shame.

"We'll leave you alone," he said quietly. "I'm sorry we barged into your home."

The man straightened slowly, tugging on his shirt as though to erase its wrinkles and grime. He nodded. "You're welcome here," he said, looking at the boys. "Come visit anytime."

"We just may do that," Willy said. "Do you mind if we bring a friend? A pastor?"

The man thought, then nodded. "OK. Bring your friend." The Ringers started to walk away, then stopped when the man spoke again. "Tell your girl . . . Jill . . . tell her I'm sorry."

Pete nodded. "We will." And then they walked into the darkness, each one struggling with his feelings.

"He was so pitiful," Willy whispered.

"Not as pitiful as we were," Pete said, his voice thick. "I was ready to clobber that guy, but he's more like a kid than a man."

"And he was just trying to protect his home," Chris added, looking around at the grave markers. "Some home," he added.

"I think we'd better give Pastor Whitehead a call when we get back to the church," Pete said, and the others nodded. They knew they had a lot to tell their friend—and a lot to apologize for.

THE END

Did you read about the vanishing visitor? If not, turn to page 116 and see what happens. Or turn back to any of the other beginnings for more adventures with the Ringers!

The girls nodded at each other. "OK, you've got a deal," Jill said. Then her eyes narrowed, and she poked a finger at Chris's chest. "But the next Ringers event, *we* get to decide what and where. Agreed?"

Chris nodded. "Agreed."

The afternoon following the overnighter, Jill was sprawled out on the couch in the living room watching TV when she heard the door open. She glanced up and watched as Chris came in, dragging his duffel bag behind him.

He looked like he'd been run over by a mail truck.

Twice.

"You look awful!" Jill commented, and Chris shot her a sour look. He stomped down the hall without a word. Jill shrugged and went back to her TV show, only to be disturbed yet again when Chris came into the room and flopped down on the couch beside her.

Jill waited for Chris to say something. And waited. And waited.

Silence.

"So, how was the all-nighter?" she asked.

More silence. And a scowl.

She crossed her arms over her chest and shifted so she could look at Chris. "OK, Martin, out with it. What happened at this glorious, all-time best monster story overnight party? You haven't acted this charming since you got a failing notice in P.E. in the third grade because you wouldn't touch the girls during square dancing."

"Yeah, well, I'd rather have been with the girls last night, that's all I can say," he muttered in a dark voice.

"Oh no, I think you can say a lot more."

He scowled again. "Let me put it this way . . . the stories stunk, and the company was worse. Seemed like all we did was argue. About *everything!* We couldn't even agree where to lay out our sleeping bags." He snorted in disgust. "That was one wasted night."

"What happened? You guys always have a good time when you're together. Or at least you usually do."

"I know. That's what made this so frustrating. It was like we all decided to be as rotten to each other as we could be." He slanted a look at her. "I guess we needed you girls there to straighten us out."

"Yeah, right," Jill said. "Like you would have listened to anything we had to say."

He shook his head. "No way, we weren't listening to anyone. We were all too determined to tell the scariest, grossest story in history . . . ," he said with a shudder, "and believe me, we came up with some real contenders. One story was so bad I thought I'd ralph."

"Oh, that would have been nice. Regurgitated pizza."

Chris sat staring at the TV for a while, then he rubbed his eyes. "I hate to admit this," he said in a tired voice, "but I think you girls were actually right. I think this story thing was a rotten idea."

"Why?"

"I don't know. I guess we were so busy thinking of gross things to put in our stories, we got carried away and started acting stupid and gross, too."

"Kind of like that verse in the Bible, huh? 'Evil words come from an evil heart and defile the man who says them.'"

"Yeah, that's a good word for how we acted. 'Defiled.' Definitely."

"It's like Pastor Whitehead told us once—doing things that God dislikes is like wallowing in a mud hole. You can't do it without getting full of mud and looking awful."

Chris nodded, then fell silent. They watched TV for a while, until he rubbed his eyes. "I think I'm going to try and get some sleep," he said. "Then I've got some phone calls to make."

"Phone calls?"

"Yeah, to the guys. That verse makes last night make more sense." He looked at her and smiled in a tired way. "I talked us into jumping into the mud hole, so the least I can do is apologize to the guys. See ya later."

Jill watched as Chris walked down the hall, then she said a quick prayer that God would help the guys to get over last night.

"Next time," she said, "we'll pick a better way to spend our time."

THE END

You can make another choice too, by turning back to the beginning and making other choices!

Within seconds, the rest of the Ringers had gathered in the clearing.

"What's the deal?" Jill asked as she trotted up. "The game can't be over—it hasn't even started yet!"

Chris filled them in on what he'd seen. "Pastor Whitehead and I are going to go to the cemetery to see if we can spot the guy again. That way we can show the police where he is."

"Can we come, too?" Sam asked.

"We'll all go to the cemetery entrance," Pastor Whitehead said, nodding, "to meet the police. Then Chris and I will go to where he saw the man. I don't intend to actually search the cemetery. I just want to see if there's anyone still around."

As quietly as they could, the group made their way to the cemetery entrance. With another caution about being quiet and waiting for the police, Pastor Whitehead told Chris to show him where he'd seen the man. Chris picked his way through the trees, then came to the spot. His eyes widened in alarm.

The man was still there!

Chris motioned to Pastor Whitehead, who came up behind him and peered into the darkness. The form was moving slowly, but not as though it was going anywhere.

Instead, it seemed to be stooping over something from time to time, then straightening up again and standing.

Chris looked at Pastor Whitehead and saw a strange look on his face—almost as though he recognized the marauder!

"Come on," whispered Pastor Whitehead, and he started to move back toward the Common.

Chris hesitated.

CHOICE ➡

If Chris follows Pastor Whitehead and returns to the Common, turn to page 77.

If Chris waits, turn to page 45.

I dunno, Chris," Jim said, frowning. "I think 'or what' fits you better than 'brilliant.'"

Chris stopped dancing around. "What's that supposed to mean?" Why did people always have to try and spoil his great ideas?

"Nothin'! I just don't think sitting around telling spook stories is all that exciting." Jim was getting a little defensive himself now. "I mean, there are lots of better things to do than that."

Chris raised his eyebrows. "Oh? Such as what, Mr. I've-Got-a-Better-Idea?"

"Such as . . ." Jim frantically searched his mind for an idea. Then his face lit up. "Such as catching the Midnight Marauder!" he said triumphantly.

"The midnight what?"

Jim grinned. He could tell from the look on Chris's face that he was not only interested, he was dying to know what Jim was talking about. He just shrugged and yawned.

"Oh, nothin'. It's just something I read about in the paper. But it's not nearly as exciting as telling ghost stories, so just never mind. . . ." He let his voice trail off in a bored manner and shrugged again.

"OK, OK, I surrender," Chris said, holding his hands up. "You are the all-time master of great ideas, and I am merely a worthless underling with no imagination. Are you happy now?"

"Well, just so you know who the *real* genius around here is—"

"Don't push it, Bozo Breath," Chris muttered through clenched teeth. "Now spill it, what are you talking about?"

Jim crossed his arms and looked at his friend. For once it was nice to have the upper hand. Maybe he wouldn't tell Chris about the marauder after all. Maybe he'd just draw the agony out and let the guy suffer for a while. If there was one thing that drove Chris Martin crazy, it was not knowing what was going on.

It would serve him right if I just don't tell! Jim thought.

If Jim keeps his secret, turn to page 85.

If he tells Chris about the marauder, turn to page 141.

Just then a piece of paper on his desk caught his attention. "Yes!" he said triumphantly, then jumped up to get it. Narrowing his eyes in deep thought, he read out loud:

" 'Brilliant Ideas for Things to Do. One: Read your new book!!!' " His lip curled in disgust. So much for that burst of genius. " 'Two: Meet the gang for ice cream. Three: Go to the movies. Four: Hang out at the mall. Five: Play computer games. Six: Walk the dog. Seven: Take out the garbage'. . . ."

He stopped, frowning. *Take out the garbage?* Had he really written that down? He looked again. Yep. It was there, in his very own handwriting. He peered at himself in the mirror. "You're pitiful," he said with a sigh.

As though to signal its agreement, the phone rang and he jumped to answer it. With any luck, it was someone with some great thing to do. Right now he'd go for anything as long as it got him out of the house and away from his mom.

"Hello?"

"Chris? It's Jim."

"Jim! Hey, buddy! Great to hear from you! So what exciting thing is on your mind? Whatever it is, I'm up for it. I'm ready. When do we leave?" Chris knew he was babbling, but he couldn't help it. He could hear the garbage calling his name. . . .

"Uh, well, OK," Jim's voice sounded a little confused. "Meet me at the church in ten minutes."

ALL RIGHT! Jim *did* have a plan. Chris had known his friend wouldn't let him down. That old garbage could just take itself out to the Dumpster!

"Great!" he said. "I'll be there." He hung up, grabbed his coat, and sailed out of his room. He ran down the hall and reached for the doorknob on the door to the apartment.

"Chris? Is that you?" his mom called from the kitchen. He turned and looked at her, but he avoided meeting her eyes.

"Uh, yeah. Jim called and wanted to do something, so I'm going over to the church."

His mom stepped into the entryway. She was wiping her hands on a dishtowel, and Chris could tell from the way she stood she was still upset about their fight. He glanced at her face.

Rats! Big mistake. The hurt was still there in her eyes, as was the concern that he knew was for him.

"Chris," she said in a quiet voice, "I'd like to talk before you leave."

CHOICE ➤

If Chris agrees to talk, go to page 83.

If he leaves without talking with his mom, turn to page 50.

Well, you guys may be scared to speak up, but I'm not!" Chris said finally. "I want to tell scary stories." He punched Sam in the arm.

"Uh, yeah," Sam agreed slowly. "Me, too. I want them to be so scary they penetrate our fibers."

Jill grimaced. "I think you guys just don't want to admit it's kind of a dumb idea. I mean, what's the point?"

"The point is that you're a chicken!" Chris retorted.

Color surged into Jill's face, but Tina jumped in before she could respond. Good thing, too, because she was set to really let Chris have it. He was a fine one to be calling her chicken! He'd obviously forgotten that they were cousins, and that they'd been together the first time they'd watched *The Wizard of Oz,* and that it was Jill who finally talked Chris into coming out from under the sofa after he dove for cover during the flying monkey scene. . . .

"Come on, you guys," Tina said. "I'm not trying to start a fight."

"Then what are you doing, Tina?" Sam asked. She sighed and sat back in her chair. Time to see if honesty really was the best policy.

"I guess I'm letting you guys know that I don't want to do this."

"How come?" Chris asked, and Tina was grateful that he didn't sound mad, but just curious.

"Well, for one thing, I don't like being scared." Jill nodded in agreement. "And for another thing, I'm not so sure the Ringers should be doing this." Chris looked like he wanted to argue, but he just clamped his lips shut and tried to listen. Tina bit her lip, then pressed on.

"I mean, the whole reason we formed our group was to be Ringers for Christ, right?" There were nods and sounds of agreement around the room. "OK, then how many of you think Jesus would sit around and tell ghost stories?"

The room was quiet.

"Well . . . but what if he came into the room when people were doing that? He wouldn't have told them to quit, would he? Not if they were just having fun?" Chris asked.

"I don't know," Tina admitted. "But I do know that the Bible says we're supposed to think about things that are good and lovely and pure."

"Right, and I was just reading in Matthew last night," Jill added, "and it says that a good person's words show that there's good inside of him, not evil. And," she said, looking at Chris, "it says that we will have to 'give account on Judgment Day for every idle word you speak.'"

"'Give account'?" Sam echoed.

"You know, report what you said and explain it."

"Oh." He looked somewhat uncomfortable at that. "So if we sit around and tell stories about ghosts and witches and vampires—"

"We'll have to explain to God someday why we were so interested in those things," Chris finished for him.

"No thanks," Jim muttered, trying to picture that.

"I'd rather eat bark for breakfast," said Sam.

Chris nodded. "Yeah, that would be a major pain."

Sam grinned. "Maybe, unless you boiled the bark. Then it would be kind of soggy, like Corn Flakes get when you let them soak too long."

Chris shook his head. "I meant explaining to God would be . . . oh, forget it." He looked at the others. "OK, so let's vote. All in favor of trashing the contest?" All the Ringers raised their hands.

"Right. It's outta here." He looked around the room again, a little smile on his face. "So, who's the Einstein that's gonna give us a replacement idea for the sleepover?"

"Well, *I'm* the Einstein in this group," piped in Sam. "But I'll let the rest of you offer your puny ideas as well."

Everyone grabbed something to throw at Sam, who covered his head, laughing. Within minutes, the room was alive with chatter and laughter. Tina settled back, happy. Whatever they did now, she was pretty sure it was going to be OK.

"Thanks, God," she whispered.

THE END

Scary stories or not, the Ringers still have some wild adventures at the sleepover! Turn to another choice, and see what happens when they encounter the Midnight Marauder, or when Jill ends up all alone in the cemetery at night, or when . . . well, just turn back and see for yourself what's in store!

Or, turn to page 142.

Jill heard the whistle blasts loud and clear. She frowned, started to head for the clearing, then paused.

"It would be just like Pete to bring along one of Chris's whistles," she muttered. "Then he could trick the rest of us into coming out and knock us all out of the game! On the other hand, what if it's Pastor Whitehead . . . ?"

She stood, undecided, until she heard someone call her name. Glancing to the right, she saw Tina trotting toward her.

"So, what do you think we should do?" Tina asked. "Weren't we supposed to return when we heard a bunch of whistle blasts?"

"How do we know it isn't a trick?" Jill asked, and Tina looked thoughtful.

"Well, I guess we don't. But we can sneak our way toward the clearing and see if Gramps is waiting for us. If he is, we know it's not a trick."

Jill agreed. "Lead on!"

Willy made his way back to the clearing when he heard the whistles. He stood cautiously behind a tree, peering at Pastor Whitehead and Chris and Sam. They were standing there, watching the woods around them. Just then, Pete came walking up.

"Boy, Sam, you're good!" he said, grinning.

138

Sam frowned. "What do you mean?"

"You won the game without firing a shot at any of us. You'll have to teach me how to do that!"

Sam laughed and Chris shook his head. "Forget the game!" he said. "I saw the marauder!"

At that, Jill, Tina, and Willy all came pouring out of the woods. "You saw *what?*" Willy exclaimed, and Chris grinned and looked at Pastor Whitehead.

"Well, the Ringers all seem to be here now. So, what do we do?"

"We go to the cemetery entrance to wait for the police," Pastor Whitehead said, ignoring the disappointed looks all around him. The Ringers followed him to the wrought-iron gate, where he told them to wait while Chris showed him where he'd seen the marauder.

Within minutes, Chris and Pastor Whitehead had reached the spot and peered toward the cemetery. Chris's eyes widened in alarm.

The marauder was still there!

CHOICE

Turn to page 77.

She couldn't do it. She just couldn't tattle.

"Uh, well, I'm not sure . . ."

Her grandfather looked at her curiously.

"I mean, I don't know if I'm going."

"Oh?" he asked. "Why is that?"

"Well, uh, I'm just not real big on overnighters. You know, everybody stays up and goofs off and the guys put slimy stuff in your sleeping bag and you never get any sleep. . . ." She realized she was babbling, and she shut up. Then she finished in a rush, "Besides, the church is kind of spooky when it's all dark."

Pastor Whitehead tilted his head to one side, watching her thoughtfully. "I know what you mean, honey," he said. "It's a big old building, and it creaks and groans a lot. And that can be kind of scary at night." She nodded silently in agreement. "But there's something you can keep in mind that may help."

"What's that?"

He smiled. "The church isn't just any old building. It's the place we go to worship God, even with all its creaks and groans. And there are lots of things there to remind you of God's presence, like the carvings of the lion and the lamb on the doors, and the stained glass windows . . ."

". . . and the Bible on the altar, and the cross at the front," Tina added. She leaned over and hugged her grandfather. "Thanks, Gramps," she whispered. "You're right. It does help to think about those things."

He hugged her back and planted a kiss on her cheek. "Just remember, sweetie: It doesn't matter where you are. God is right there with you."

She nodded, snuggling against him, feeling safe and protected.

Maybe it didn't matter what the Ringers did at the overnighter. Like Gramps had said, God would be with them. And he wouldn't let them do something wrong.

Would he?

She buried her face in her grandfather's chest, wishing she could make up her mind and that she wasn't so confused and that she'd been totally honest with her grandfather . . . and that the squirmy feeling she had deep down in her insides would just go away.

CHOICE ⇒

If Tina goes to the overnight with the gang, turn to page 116.

If she refuses, turn to page 25.

Well, I'd like to drive you even crazier than you already are," Jim said. "But I've heard it's Be Kind to Animals Day, so here." With that, he dug into his pocket and handed Chris a newspaper clipping.

Chris read it with increasing interest, then looked at Jim, with eyes that gleamed with excitement.

"Jim, my boy, you've done it again. This is a job for the Ringers, and I know exactly when and where to tell them about it!"

CHOICE

Turn to page 15.

142

Ghost stories, Lazer Tag, and a cemetery can combine for a pretty adventurous sleepover, don't you think? If you haven't followed all the choices the Ringers *could* have made, turn back to the beginning and try some others. Or, if you're *really* crazy, jump right into the middle and see if you can follow what's going on!

The Ringers have a lot of adventures like this. Have you gone on them all? Check out the other books in this series—you'll be amazed at what a gang of fourteen-year-old "Ringers" for Jesus can get into . . . and learn!

Karen Ball is editor and line manager for children's, youth, and fiction books at Tyndale House Publishers. She has also served as a youth sponsor at her church. Karen lives with her husband, Don, and their Siberian husky and ferret, in Aurora, Illinois.